CLASSIC
Fairy Tales

FROM HANS CHRISTIAN ANDERSEN
AND THE BROTHERS GRIMM

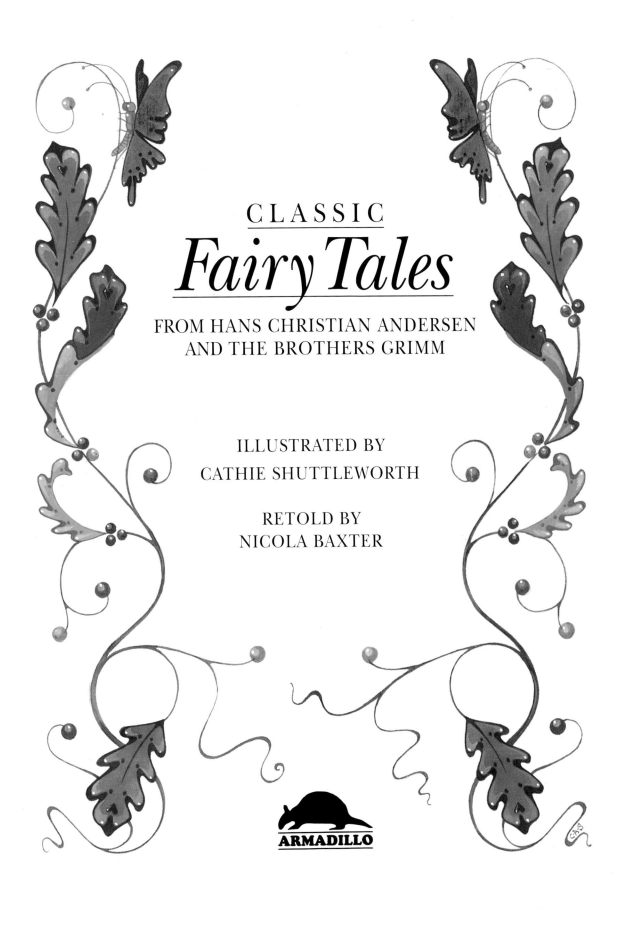

CLASSIC
Fairy Tales

FROM HANS CHRISTIAN ANDERSEN
AND THE BROTHERS GRIMM

ILLUSTRATED BY
CATHIE SHUTTLEWORTH

RETOLD BY
NICOLA BAXTER

ARMADILLO

This edition published in 2002 by Armadillo Books
An imprint of Bookmart Limited
Blaby Road, Wigston
Leicestershire, LE18 4SE, England

ISBN 1-84322-131-4

3 5 7 9 10 8 6 4 2

Previously published as
Fairy Tales from Hans Christian Andersen and
Fairy Tales from the Brothers Grimm

Produced for Bookmart by
Nicola Baxter
PO Box 215, Framingham Earl
Norwich NR14 7UR

Printed in Singapore

HANS CHRISTIAN ANDERSEN

Hans Christian Andersen, the Danish storyteller, was born in 1805. Although he was the son of a poor shoemaker, he longed to make his living by writing. After many struggles, he finally became known as a poet, but today it is his fairy tales that are best loved.

Perhaps the secret of Andersen's success is that he wrote his stories, as he told a friend, as if he were telling them to a child.

Each time a story is told, it changes a little, to suit its teller and its audience. Everyone has a different idea about why the characters act as they do and which part of the story is most interesting. So these stories are not *exactly* as Hans Christian Andersen wrote them, over a hundred and fifty years ago and in a different language, but they are still full of strange and wonderful things. When you tell them to your own children, no doubt they will change a little more.

Pictures tell stories too from age to age;
Search low and high
To find a butterfly
Fluttering on every page.

THE BROTHERS GRIMM

Jacob Ludwig Carl Grimm was born in 1785 in Germany. His brother Wilhelm Carl came along a year later. Both brothers loved the German language and the stories that were told in it. In 1812, they published their first collection of folk and fairy tales, collected from all over Germany. Many of the stories had been told for centuries, enchanting children and adults with their mixture of magic, mystery and truths older even than the stories themselves.

The brothers went on to make other collections. Their books were soon translated and became popular in many parts of the world. Today these stories are part of a heritage of folk and fairy tales shared across borders and languages.

The world still needs storytellers today—to tell the old well-loved tales and to make up new stories. Don't forget—you can be a storyteller, too.

Pictures tell stories too from age to age;
Search if you wish
And find a fish
Swimming on every page.

CONTENTS

FAIRY TALES FROM
HANS CHRISTIAN ANDERSEN 9

CONTENTS

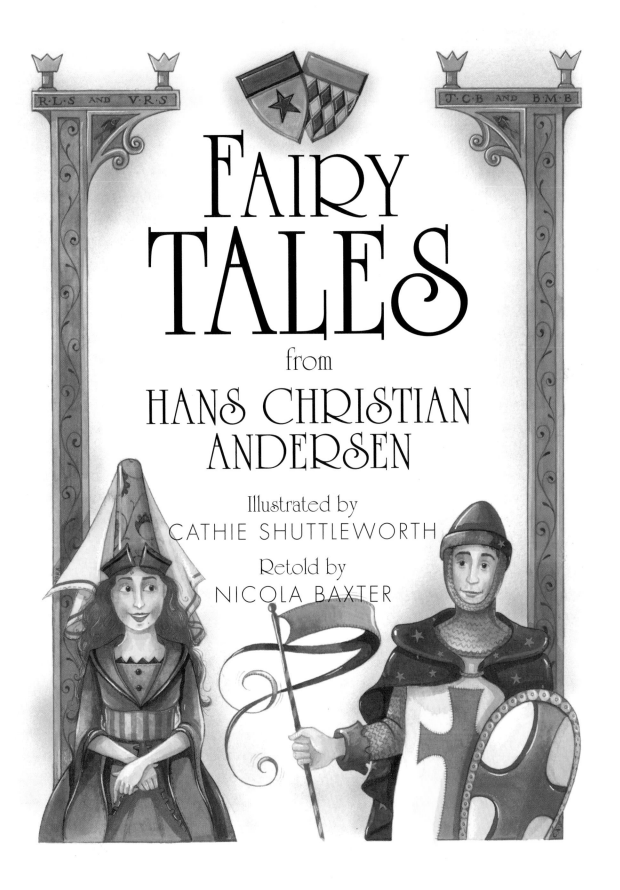

FAIRY TALES

from

HANS CHRISTIAN ANDERSEN

Illustrated by
CATHIE SHUTTLEWORTH

Retold by
NICOLA BAXTER

R·L·S AND V·R·S

J·C·B AND B·M·B

THE LITTLE MERMAID

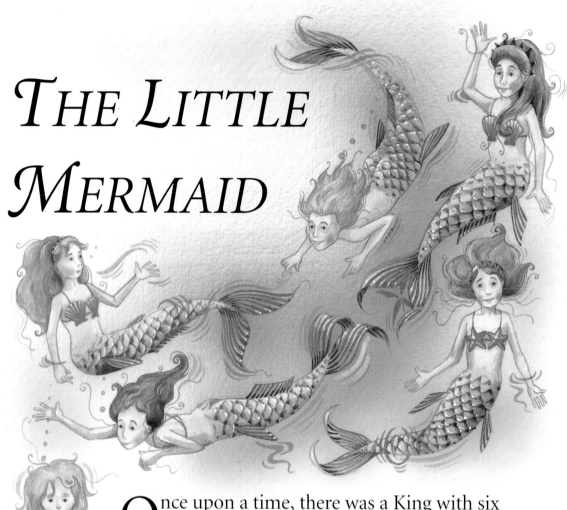

Once upon a time, there was a King with six beautiful daughters, but he was not a King of the human world. His lands lay far, far below the waves, where fish flash like little jewels among the reefs and craggy rocks.

The King and the six Princesses lived in a wonderful palace, made of glowing coral and gleaming shells. The girls' mother had died, but their grandmother took good care of them. Of all the Princesses, the youngest was the most beautiful. Her long hair floated around her like a golden cloud, and her tail shimmered with blue, green, and silver.

If there was one thing that the Princesses loved above all, it was to hear their grandmother tell them stories of the land above the waves. There, she told them, human beings walked on strange things called legs. And extraordinary fish swam through the air, flapping their long fins.

The more the old merwoman talked of this strange world, the more the youngest mermaid longed to see it.

"When you are fifteen," her grandmother promised, "you shall go."

When the eldest Princess was old enough, she swam to the surface, returning the next day to tell of the wonderful things she had seen.

"There are glittering cities," she said, "with twinkling lights and the sound of humans laughing. And there are huge ships, as large as palaces, that sail across the sea in the sunshine."

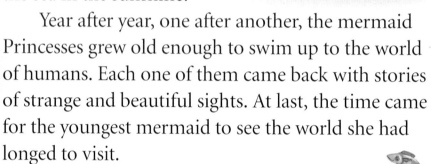

Year after year, one after another, the mermaid Princesses grew old enough to swim up to the world of humans. Each one of them came back with stories of strange and beautiful sights. At last, the time came for the youngest mermaid to see the world she had longed to visit.

As she rose to the surface for the first time, the sun was just setting, tingeing the sky with pink and gold. Nearby, a fine ship was drifting gently, for there was very little wind. As the little mermaid watched, a handsome Prince came onto the deck and looked out across the sea. He did not know that he was being watched, or that the little mermaid could not take her eyes from his face.

Darkness fell, and the ship began to toss as the wind rose. A dreadful storm wrenched away the sails and the rigging, and huge waves crashed onto the deck, tearing apart the planks. As the ship sank, the little mermaid caught sight of the Prince, struggling in the water.

Before long, the Prince closed his eyes, too tired to stay afloat any longer. But the little mermaid held up his head and guided him gently to shore. When morning came, the wind dropped and the sun rose. The little mermaid stayed near the shore, so that she could watch over the sleeping Prince.

Before long, some girls from the nearby town came down to the sea. The Prince woke as they bent over him on the sand, smiling as they helped him away. Only the little mermaid felt sad. She feared that she would never see him again.

After that, the little mermaid often rose to the surface, eager for a sight of the Prince. She watched his beautiful palace from the nearby sea and sometimes saw him walking among his courtiers. Yet she grew sadder and sadder, until she could not bear it any more. She decided to go to see the Water Witch.

The Water Witch lived in a deep, dark part of the ocean, where water snakes writhed in the cold water. When she saw the little mermaid, she laughed.

"I know why you have come," she said. "You want to go and live in the human world, so that you can be near the Prince. You want me to turn your mermaid's tail into human legs, ugly as they are. But do you know the price you will have to pay?"

"No," whispered the Princess, "but I will pay it gladly to be human."

"I shall need your voice, with which you sing so sweetly," said the witch. "Then I can turn you into a human girl, as lovely as any that walks on Earth. But remember, if the Prince does not love you with all his heart and take you for his wife, you will turn into sea foam and be lost forever. You can never return to your home beneath the waves."

"Hurry," said the mermaid. "I have already decided."

So the Water Witch gave the little mermaid a potion to drink. The Princess rose to the surface and swam beneath the Prince's palace. A terrible sadness overwhelmed her as she drank the potion, for she knew how much she was leaving behind.

But that sadness was forgotten when she stood for the first time before the Prince she loved. He at once wanted to meet the beautiful stranger and, although she could not speak to him, he soon found that he could not bear to be apart from her, but kept her always by his side.

The little mermaid loved the young man more each day, but he never thought of marrying her. "You remind me of a girl who once saved me from drowning," he said. "She is the only one I could ever really love." The poor little mermaid could not tell him that he had already met her.

Months passed, and the Prince's mother and father urged him to find a bride. At last he agreed to meet a Princess in a nearby country. Of course, the little mermaid went with him on the royal ship, although she felt as if her heart were breaking.

When the Prince stepped on shore and met the new Princess for the first time, he was so dazzled by her beauty that he believed he was meeting the girl who had saved him from the sea. "It is you!" he cried. "I have found the girl I shall love for the rest of my life."

Preparations for the wedding were made at once. It was a magnificent affair, with flowers and silks and jewels. Everyone cheered with joy to see the happy pair. Only the little mermaid was silent, and her tears fell unseen.

That night, as the Prince and his bride were guided to their cabin on the royal ship, the little mermaid stood on deck and gazed at the dark water. At dawn, she would be turned into foam, never to see, or hear, or love again.

But as she stood there, the little mermaid's sisters rose to the surface of the water. Their flowing hair was cut short.

"We gave it to the Water Witch," they said, "in return for this knife. If you kill the Prince tonight, you will be free of the spell and can return to live with us in your home under the sea."

The little mermaid took the knife, but when she stood above the sleeping Prince, she knew that she could never harm him. Weeping, she flung the knife away and plunged into the sea.

But instead of
turning into foam, the
little mermaid found
herself floating in the air,
the ship sailing on far
below. Around her were
lovely creatures made of
golden light.

"We are the daughters
of the air," they said.
"By doing kind acts
for others, we gain
happiness ourselves.
You belong with us,
little mermaid,
where you can
be happy
at last."

As the little mermaid rose into the sunshine, she
looked down at the Prince and his bride, standing on
the deck of the ship. And for the first time in a long,
long while, she smiled.

THUMBELINA

Sometimes wishes do come true. There was once a woman who longed above everything else to have a little girl of her own. She went to a wise old woman to ask for advice.

"I want so much to have a little tiny girl to care for," she told the old woman.

"That is easy, my dear," said the old woman. "Take this barley seed and plant it in a pot. It is no ordinary seed, as you will see."

So the woman went home and planted the seed. Almost at once, a green shoot appeared. It quickly grew into a strong plant, with one large bud. When the bud opened, there was a beautiful red and yellow flower, a little like a tulip.

The astonished woman bent and kissed the lovely petals, and at that very moment, the flower opened. In the middle sat a little tiny girl, perfect in every way.

Because she was no bigger than the woman's thumb, she was called Thumbelina.

There never was a little girl who was loved so much or cared for so well. She had a walnut shell for a cradle and rose leaves for a blanket, while violet flowers made a pretty pillow for her head.

As her mother worked around the house during the day, Thumbelina played on the table. She had a shallow dish of water, with a lily leaf in the middle, and she loved to row herself back and forth in the sunlight from the open window. As she rowed, she sang so sweetly that even the birds outside stopped to listen to her.

So Thumbelina was happy, until one night a mother toad hopped through the window and saw the tiny girl in her pretty bed.

"She would make a beautiful wife for my son," thought the toad, and she picked up the sleeping girl and carried her back to the riverbank.

So that Thumbelina could not escape, the toad put her on a lily leaf in the middle of the river. The little girl was not frightened, for she remembered her days playing on the table, but she did want to go home, and she did not want to marry the toad's son.

When the toad hopped away to make a house for her son in the reeds, Thumbelina sat on her leaf and sobbed. A little fish heard her crying and popped up his head.

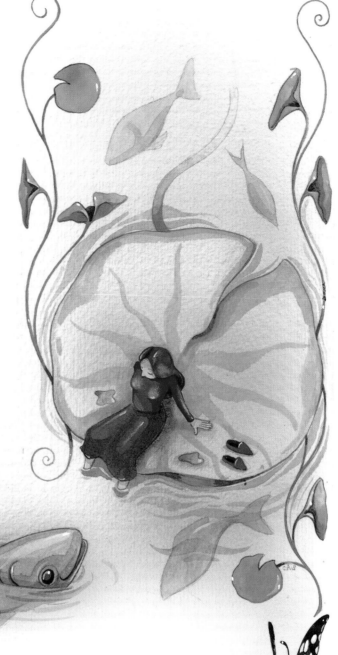

"You cannot marry that ugly old toad," he said. And he bit through the stem of the lily leaf so that it went floating down the river.

Thumbelina felt happier now. She passed many beautiful places, and a butterfly flew down to visit her.

But Thumbelina's troubles were not over. A large black beetle seized her and carried her up into a tree. The beetle thought she was pretty, but when his friends came, they laughed. "She is so ugly!" they said. "She only has two legs! Look!"

The beetle carried Thumbelina down to a flowery meadow and left her there. He could not bear to hear his friends laugh at him. And so, Thumbelina passed the summer quite happily, drinking nectar from the flowers and playing with her friends the butterflies.

But gradually, the days began to grow shorter. Winter was coming, and the nights were cold. Thumbelina knew that she could not survive the winter without a home to live in. As the first flakes of snow began to fall, she wrapped herself in a dry leaf and set off to find shelter.

Just as the shivering girl began to lose hope, she met a busy little mouse. "You can stay with me, in my little house," said the mouse kindly.

Thumbelina was happy in the snug little home, until the mouse's friend came to visit. He was a mole who lived underground, and he soon fell in love with Thumbelina and wanted to marry her.

"You are lucky," said the mouse. "The mole is rich. You will never want for anything again."

One day, the mole took Thumbelina to see his underground home. As they walked along a dark passageway, the mole warned her, "Be careful here. Something has died and is lying in the way."

Thumbelina knelt down. She felt that it was a beautiful bird, and his little heart was still feebly beating.

Thumbelina took care of the bird, and by spring, it was ready to fly away to join its friends. Thumbelina watched it fly away, and wished that she too could escape. She knew that when winter came again, she would have to marry the mole and live underground for the rest of her life.

Summer passed again, and autumn leaves were rustling around her feet as Thumbelina stood and looked at the blue sky for the last time. She felt a terrible sadness pressing down on her.

Just then, a voice from above called to her. "Come with me! I'm flying to a warmer country for the winter. You will love it there." It was the bird she had rescued almost a year before!

In no time at all, Thumbelina was sitting on the bird's back, soaring over fields and cities. The bird flew over mountains, lakes, and the stormy sea. At last he came to rest in a warm, sunny country, where orange trees grew and the air was full of the scent of beautiful flowers.

The swallow set Thumbelina down on a leaf among the flowers. You can imagine how surprised she was to see a little man, no bigger than herself, sitting among the petals.

"Welcome to my country," he said. "I am the Prince of all the flower people. We are so happy to see you, we will call you Maia."

So the little girl was happy at last. She fell in love with the Prince and married him, and her lovely voice was often heard singing sweetly in the scented air.

THE EMPEROR'S NEW CLOTHES

Some Emperors like nothing better than to wage war on three nearby kingdoms before breakfast. Some love to build beautiful castles and palaces, each one bigger and better than the last. But the Emperor in this story had a more unusual passion: he loved clothes. It was well known that the Emperor spent most of the day trying on one costume after another to find which was most flattering to the (rather generous) royal figure.

One day there came to the court a pair of rascals intent on making a little money and living an easy life. They let it be known that they were weavers—and not just ordinary ones. "The cloth that we weave," they said, "is so extraordinarily fine, and its pattern is so rare and intricate, that only the most intelligent and refined people can see it."

Before long, news of the two so-called weavers reached the ears of the Emperor. "How very useful," he said to himself. "If I wore a suit of that cloth, I would be able to tell at once which of my ministers were too stupid and ill bred for their jobs." So he summoned the weavers before him.

When they arrived at the court, the two mischief makers bowed low. "What is Your Imperial Highness's pleasure?" they asked.

"I would like a suit made entirely of your famous cloth," declared the Emperor, "and I would like it by the end of the week!"

"No problem at all," replied the weavers reassuringly. "Now, if we could just take a few measurements…. My, my, Your Highness has the figure of a man of … *ahem* … twenty!"

Next the weavers ordered bales of costly silk and gold thread, to weave, they said, into their famous cloth. They had two enormous looms set up in a comfortable room. All day long they sat in front of the looms, pretending to weave. Of course, the looms were completely empty.

The Emperor was anxious to see how his suit was coming along, but although he knew that he was the cleverest man in the land, he was just a little worried that he might not be able to see the cloth.

The Emperor thought long and hard (in fact, surprisingly long and hard for the cleverest man in the land) until he had an idea.

"Summon my Chief Minister!" he cried. "He can report to me on the cloth the weavers are making for me."

Well, the Chief Minister couldn't see the cloth either. But he was very worried that the Emperor might dismiss him if he was one of those unfortunate people who were too stupid to see it. "It's absolutely perfect for Your Highness," he reported. "I can honestly say that I have never seen anything to match it."

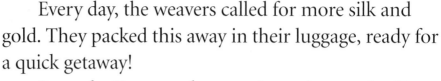

Every day, the weavers called for more silk and gold. They packed this away in their luggage, ready for a quick getaway!

Soon the Emperor became impatient again. He sent his Chancellor to inspect the work. Once again, the poor man could see nothing at all, but he did not want to lose his job. "It is beyond compare," he declared. "Your Highness will be really delighted."

At last the Emperor could bear it no longer. He hurried along to the room where the weavers were working and flung open the doors.

The weavers, who had heard the swish of royal robes in the corridor, were very busy at their looms. Their hands darted backward and forward, holding … absolutely nothing!

The Emperor stopped dead. It was his worst nightmare! Only he, of all his court, was too stupid to see the wonderful cloth. His throat felt dry and his voice quavered as he announced, "The Chief Minister and the Chancellor were too faint in their praise. This cloth is truly too beautiful for words!"

At the end of the week there was to be a Grand Procession. Naturally, it was expected that the Emperor would wear clothes of the famous new cloth, of which the whole empire had heard. The weavers were busy night and day, cutting thin air with huge pairs of scissors, sewing with invisible thread, and pretending to sew on buttons and braid. When they were tired of this, they smiled at each other and said, "There! A costume fit for an Emperor!"

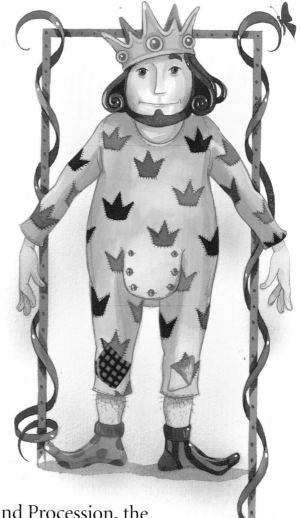

On the morning of the Grand Procession, the Emperor stood in his underwear while the weavers helped him on with his clothes. He agreed with everything they had to say about the cut and the cloth. By the time he had walked up and down a few times, so that the weavers, as they said, could see how well the train draped, he had persuaded himself that he could almost see the costume, and that it was very fine indeed.

So it was that the Emperor walked proudly out at the head of his royal regiment wearing only his second-best pair of royal underwear.

At first, there was a stunned silence from the crowd lining the streets. But everyone had heard that only clever people could see the clothes, so first one and then another spectator cried out, "Wonderful! Superb!" as the Emperor passed. Before long, almost everyone was applauding and cheering. The Emperor felt on top of the world.

Now, it sometimes happens when everyone is
making a lot of noise that there is suddenly a brief
silence, and one of these silences happened just as the
Emperor reached the Great Square. In that moment of
quiet, the voice of a little boy could be heard clearly all
around the square. "But Mother," he cried, "the
Emperor isn't wearing any clothes!"

In that dreadful moment, the whole crowd
realized that it was true, and they had been as silly as
the Emperor. One by one, the people began to laugh.
The Emperor struggled to remain dignified for a
second. Then, scooping his imaginary train over one
arm, he ran in a most unroyal way back to the palace.

It is said that the Emperor never was quite so vain
about clothes after that, and perhaps he had the
wicked weavers to thank for it. But those two rascals
had become as invisible as the Emperor's famous
costume and were never seen again.

THE PRINCESS AND THE PEA

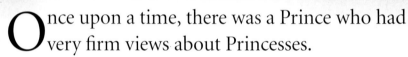

O nce upon a time, there was a Prince who had very firm views about Princesses.

"Many of them are simply not Princesses," he said airily.

"My dear, whatever do you mean?" asked his mother the Queen. "Of course they are real Princesses. What about that perfectly charming girl we met last week?"

"She spoke unkindly to her maid," said the Prince.

"Yes, yes, my boy, but Princess Pearl from Argentia was sweetness itself, surely," urged the King.

"She was *silly*," said the Prince.

"But Princess Petronella, so delightful, so accomplished, so refreshing," cried the King and Queen together.

"She was not a *real* Princess at all," said the Prince. "She talked all the time and never listened to a word anyone else said. Real Princesses are … well, they're … that is, they seem … oh, I don't know!"

"I do wish he could meet someone and settle down," sighed the King, as the Prince rushed from the room. "But how are we ever to be sure that a girl is a real Princess? Nowadays, it's so difficult to be sure. I believe I married the last real Princess myself!"

"My dear," said the Queen with a smile, "if the right girl comes along, I know exactly how to make sure that she is what she seems. Just leave it to me."

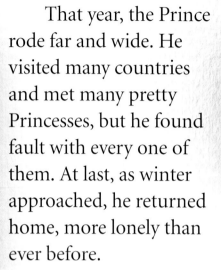

That year, the Prince rode far and wide. He visited many countries and met many pretty Princesses, but he found fault with every one of them. At last, as winter approached, he returned home, more lonely than ever before.

But one night, as the King and Queen and the Prince sat in front of a roaring fire, there came a deafening knocking at the door of the castle.

"Some poor fellow is out in the storm," said the King. "We must let him in to warm himself."

"But, my dear," his wife protested, "we don't know who it is."

But the King was already striding toward the door. The wind blew so hard that he could hardly stand upright as he pulled it open.

Outside in the courtyard stood a rain-drenched figure. The King had to peer more closely to see that it was not a man at all, but a young girl, shivering in a thin cloak.

"My dear child," cried the King. "Come in at once! Whatever can you be doing out and about on a night like this?"

"My carriage overturned, and I was forced to go in search of shelter," replied the girl, as she came inside. "And you would be surprised how few people are prepared to help a real Princess when she knocks on their door."

The King and Queen exchanged a glance. "Did you say a *real* Princess?" asked the King.

"Of course," his visitor replied. "My father is a King, after all."

"Well, that is interesting," said the King. "I wonder, have you met my son, the Prince?"

The Prince hurried forward at once to kiss the Princess's dainty hand. In fact, he had been unable to take his eyes off the visitor since she first began to drip onto the royal carpet!

"I will have a room prepared for you at once," said the Queen, hurrying from the room.

An hour later, the Princess was tucked up in her room, and the Prince wandered off to walk up and down the corridors, lost in a warm glow of imagining.

The King could not wait to consult his wife.

"Well?" he whispered. "What do you think? The boy seems rather taken with her, but is she the real thing?"

"We'll soon know about that," said the Queen. "I have put twenty mattresses on her bed. Below the bottom mattress I have placed a dried pea. Now we shall see what we shall see."

"Ah," said the King, "the old pea trick, eh?" Though in truth he had not the faintest idea what the Queen was talking about.

Next morning, the members of the royal family were—for different reasons—not at all able to concentrate on their breakfast. Things did not improve when their visitor entered the room.

As the Prince hurried to find the pretty girl a chair, the Queen leaned forward eagerly.

"My dear," she said, "I do hope you had a quiet and restful night."

"I'm afraid not," replied the girl, "although you made me so welcome and comfortable. Yet I tossed and turned all night long, and this morning I am black and blue. It's as though there was a boulder under my mattresses."

At that the Queen beamed at her son. "Here," she said, "is a real Princess, my boy. Only a girl with truly royal blood would have skin so tender that she could feel a tiny pea through twenty mattresses. You have my blessing."

"And mine," cried the King, jumping up to clap his son on the shoulder.

Luckily, it was soon discovered that the Princess had fallen as much in love with the Prince as he had with her. They were married soon after, amid great rejoicing.

Well, that was many years ago now, but the royal museum still contains a rather wrinkled green exhibit. You can see it for yourself, if you care to visit.

THE SNOW QUEEN

Our story begins with a mirror owned by a wicked sorcerer. To his delight, the mirror made everything look ugly and twisted, no matter how beautiful it really was. When people looked in the mirror, they said to themselves, "How stupid I've been. Everything is horrid, and it's not worth trying to be good or kind." One day, the mirror broke, and thousands of tiny pieces went flying across the world. Some were so small that people didn't feel it when a tiny fragment flew into their eyes. They only noticed that everything suddenly looked spoiled and dirty. Worse still were the tiny sharp slivers that flew into people's hearts. They turned them to ice, so that they could not feel love and happiness anymore.

Meanwhile, a little girl and boy who lived opposite each other were playing happily high above the busy street. Their houses were built so that each floor was wider than the one below, so the top of the houses almost touched. There were window boxes on the top floor, in which flowers and roses had been planted. In the summer, the little girl, who was called Gerda, and the little boy, who was called Kay, played together in their tiny garden, while the roses twined above them.

In the winter, when the windows were shut, they had to run down all the stairs in the houses to meet indoors. They watched the snowflakes swirling through the window like a flock of white bees.

"There is a Queen of the Snow just as there is a Queen Bee," said Grandmother. "She is the biggest snowflake, whirling in the storm."

That evening, when Kay was getting ready for bed, he peered through the window and saw one large snowflake landing on the window box. Before his eyes, it seemed to grow into a beautiful woman, dressed all in white. Her eyes shone like stars, and she seemed to shimmer like ice. Kay knew that she was the Snow Queen. He thought she was the loveliest person he had ever seen. But her eyes were cold, and when she beckoned to the little boy, he turned away from the window and snuggled down in his warm bed. For a second, it seemed as if the shadow of a big black bird flew across the window.

The next day, when Kay and Gerda were playing outside, Kay suddenly gave a little cry.

"Oh," he said, "I just felt a sharp pain in my heart, as if something stabbed me, and it felt as though something flew into my eye, too. But I feel better now."

Tiny pieces of the sorcerer's mirror were now lodged in Kay's eye and heart, which was turned to ice. Seeing Gerda's worried little face, Kay spoke coldly.

"What's the matter with you, Gerda? You don't look at all pretty like that. I'm going off to play with the other boys in the square."

"But we were going to look at my new picture book," said Gerda.

"That's just for babies," shouted Kay, already halfway down the street with his little sled. It was not the real Kay talking, but the ice in his heart.

In the square, there was thick snow. As Kay sat on his toy sled, a magnificent full-sized sleigh swept into the square. It was pulled by white horses and moving like an icy wind. In a flash, Kay stretched out his hands and grabbed hold of the sleigh, so that he was pulled along behind it. Faster and faster they went, out of the city and into the whirling, white countryside.

As the sleigh flew over the fields, the snow swirled thicker around Kay. He began to be rather frightened.

At last the strange sleigh stopped, and the white figure driving it stood up. Kay could see that it was the Snow Queen, dressed in a cloak of white fur.

"Are you cold, little Kay?" she asked. "Come here under my cloak." Kay looked up at the Snow Queen and thought she was more beautiful than ever. He was no longer afraid but flew on with her in the moonlight, gazing at the twinkling stars above the sparkling snow.

Back in the city, little Gerda learned that Kay had disappeared. All through the winter she felt lost and alone, wondering where her friend had gone. Everyone said that he must be dead, but Gerda could not believe that. As soon as spring arrived, she set off to find Kay in her new red shoes.

Gerda soon reached the countryside. Before long, she saw a large orchard, full of cherry trees. There was a little house there too, with red and blue windows. Out of the house came an old woman. She wore a straw hat, covered with beautiful flowers.

Gerda was glad to see a friendly face. Soon she had told the old woman all about Kay.

"I haven't seen him," said the old woman, "but he is sure to come along sooner or later. You can stay here and wait."

In fact, the old woman really wanted to look after a little girl just like Gerda. She fed her delicious cherries and let her play in the wonderful flower garden, and she was careful to magic away all the roses, so that Gerda was not reminded of home.

But the old lady had forgotten about her hat! One day, Gerda noticed that one of the flowers on it was a beautiful rose. "Oh, no!" cried the little girl. "I have wasted so much time." It was nearly autumn, and still she had not found Kay. Without even waiting to put on her shoes, Gerda ran out of the garden and out into the wide world.

Poor Gerda's feet were soon sore, so she sat down to rest. A large raven was hopping about nearby. Not knowing which way to turn next, the little girl told him her story and asked his advice.

"I may have seen Kay," said the raven, "but he has forgotten all about you. He thinks only of the Princess."

"Is he living with a Princess?" asked Gerda.

✖   Then the raven told her about a Princess who was very clever. When she had read all the books in the castle and was bored, she decided to look for a husband. But he must on no account be a stupid man.

✖   The Princess advertised for a husband, and before long, the grand staircase of the castle was packed with young men lining up to see her. Unfortunately, when they came into her presence, all of them were too amazed by her pearl throne and the rich decorations to say a word, so the Princess sent them away.

"But what about Kay?" asked Gerda impatiently.

Then the raven told how a boy who was not afraid of anyone came along and delighted the Princess by talking with her about all the things that interested her.

"Oh, that must be Kay. He is always so clever," said Gerda. "I must get into that castle and see him!"

"I will see what I can do," cawed the raven, and he flew away.

At evening, the raven came back. "My sweetheart, who lives in the castle, will let you in through a little back door," he said. "Come quickly!"

So Gerda hurried to the castle, where another raven was waiting. She crept up the back stairs. As she did so, she felt that she almost saw swift shadows of swishing skirts and horses and soldiers flitting past. The raven explained that these were the dreams of the ladies and gentlemen sleeping inside.

At last Gerda reached the Princess's room. There, sleeping soundly, was a young man. The little girl crept closer and pulled away the cover. It wasn't Kay!

Gerda was so disappointed that she burst into tears, waking the Prince and Princess. At first she thought they would be angry, but they felt sorry for the little girl and did what they could to help her. They gave her some new boots and a golden carriage, with footmen to take her on her way.

But Gerda's adventures were not over. As she passed in her carriage through a dark forest, some robbers jumped out, pulling her from her seat. They could see that the carriage was worth a fortune. Those robbers might well have killed Gerda at once, if it hadn't been for a little robber girl, who decided to take Gerda back to the robbers' broken-down castle. There she showed Gerda her pet reindeer, but she did not seem to treat him very well.

That night Gerda found it difficult to sleep. High above her head in the rafters, some wood pigeons began to coo. "We have seen little Kay riding through the sky in the Snow Queen's sleigh," they said softly. "She was probably going to Lapland, for the snow and ice never melt there."

"That's true," said the reindeer quietly. "The Snow Queen has her summer palace near the North Pole. I know, for I was born near there."

The next morning, the little robber girl spoke to Gerda. "I heard everything last night," she said. "I will let the reindeer go if he will promise to carry you to Lapland to find Kay."

The reindeer jumped for joy, and Gerda was so happy that she cried. She climbed on the reindeer's back. Night and day they flew through the forest and mountains, until the reindeer pointed out the beautiful northern lights and told Gerda that they had arrived in Lapland.

There was a poor cottage nearby. Shivering with cold, Gerda told her story to the woman who lived there.

"You poor child," said the woman. "I'm afraid you have many miles to go yet. The Snow Queen's palace is in Finland. I will write you a note to a Finnish woman I know. She will help you when you get there."

Once again, Gerda and the reindeer flew over the snowy landscape, until they reached the Finnish woman's home. There was a huge fire inside, so that the inside of the hut was as hot as the outside was cold. The Finnish woman wore hardly any clothes because of the heat, and she immediately helped Gerda off with her coat and boots.

When she had read the note from her friend in Lapland, the Finnish woman looked at Gerda and the reindeer.

"Can't you give Gerda some special magic, so that she can defeat the Snow Queen?" asked the reindeer.

"Gerda doesn't need any special magic," said the Finnish woman. "Her good heart is all the magic she needs. Kay *is* with the Snow Queen. He is happy there because he has a heart of ice and a fragment of the sorcerer's mirror in his eye. Take Gerda out to the edge of the Snow Queen's garden and put her down by a bush with red berries."

The reindeer did as the Finnish woman suggested, although he was sorry to leave Gerda all alone in the cold snow with her bare feet.

Almost at once, Gerda was surrounded by whirling snowflakes. Some seemed ugly and twisted. They moved threateningly toward her, like soldiers. But other snowflakes, like white angels, led her on.

And so it was that Gerda came at last to the Snow Queen's palace, with its walls of snow and doors and windows of bitter winds. Only Gerda's goodness kept her warm as she walked into a huge ice chamber.

There in the middle was little Kay, moving blocks of ice around as if he was trying to solve the most important puzzle in the world.

"Oh, Kay!" cried Gerda, running toward him. Kay stood stiff and cold. He was so pale that he looked almost blue, and he did not greet the little girl who had come so far to find him.

But as Gerda threw her arms around Kay, her warm tears of joy dripped onto his face and heart, melting the ice and washing away the slivers of mirror. The warmth gradually returned to his cheeks, and he too cried at the sight of his very best friend.

Outside, the reindeer was waiting. The children began their long journey home. As they went, the snow melted and the grass and flowers smelled sweet beneath their feet. At last they saw their own city stretching out before them. Holding hands, they ran through the streets they knew so well.

It was as though nothing had changed. Grandmother still sat by the window, and the flowers and roses bloomed in the window boxes high above the street. There Gerda and Kay sat as they had sat before. They were older and wiser, but in their hearts they were children still, and all around them was warmth and light and summer.

THE EMPEROR AND THE NIGHTINGALE

Long ago, the great empire of China had a mighty Emperor. His magnificent palace was built of fragile porcelain and stood in the most beautiful garden the world has ever seen. Not only were the flowers exquisite, but the gardeners had hung tiny silver bells among them, so that they tinkled little tunes among the blooms.

At the end of the gardens was a wonderful forest, and beyond the forest the deep blue sea stretched far away. It was here, at the edge of the water, that a nightingale had made its home. Sitting in the branches of a stately tree, the nightingale each evening opened her heart and sang so beautifully that even the hard-working fishermen stopped their work to hear her liquid notes.

Many strangers came to the imperial palace to gasp at the porcelain and the treasures inside. Of course, they were equally amazed by the intricate gardens and the trees beyond. But every visitor who heard the song of the nightingale could not help exclaiming, "Everything here is wonderful beyond belief, but nothing compares to the song of this magical bird."

When they returned to their own countries, some of the visitors wrote books describing the extraordinary things they had seen, and all of them ended by praising the nightingale's song above everything else.

Now the Emperor was very fond of reading books about his country, and he was especially fond of reading about his amazing palace and its grounds. He felt proud to be the owner of such magnificence. You can imagine his surprise when he first read an account that rated the nightingale's song more highly than all his costly possessions.

"Why have I never heard the song of this bird, although she lives within my grounds?" he asked his courtiers. "Bring her to me tonight, for I must hear her sing."

The courtiers had never heard of the nightingale. They ran all over the palace, searching for someone who had heard of her, but with no success.

"Perhaps the story in your book has been invented by the author, Your Imperial Highness," suggested the courtiers.

"Nonsense," said the Emperor. "You must all search harder."

The courtiers were almost at their wits' ends when they found a young maid in the Emperor's enormous kitchens.

"I have heard the nightingale sing many times, when I go down to the shore to visit my mother," she said. "It is a truly wonderful sound."

The courtiers insisted that the kitchen maid lead them to the nightingale's tree, but they themselves had no idea what her song would be like. As they walked through the forest beyond the gardens, they heard a deep, booming sound.

"What a beautiful song," they cried. "We have found the nightingale."

"No, no," said the kitchen maid. "That is a cow calling to its calf."

Next the courtiers heard a bubbling, chirping sound.

"There, that is the nightingale," they declared. "How beautiful!"

"No," replied the kitchen maid, looking at them in amazement. "That is a frog, calling across a pond."

Just then the nightingale began to sing. A ribbon of beautiful sound shimmered in the air. The kitchen maid pointed to a little brown bird on a branch.

"That is the nightingale," she said.

The courtiers were amazed that such a drab bird could make such a beautiful sound, but they invited her to the palace that evening, as the Emperor had commanded. The nightingale was astonished that she should be summoned in such a way, but she went along willingly to sing to the owner of the palace and the gardens and the forest and the sea.

The entire court gathered with the Emperor to hear the nightingale sing that evening. A special golden stand had been made for her to perch on.

As the nightingale's first notes trembled in the air, tears rolled down the Emperor's cheeks. He had never heard anything so beautiful. Everyone else in the room was equally moved. The little bird was a great success.

After that, the nightingale had to live at the palace. She had her own golden cage and twelve servants. Twice a day, she was allowed to fly around a little, but one of the servants kept hold of a silken thread attached to her leg, so she was never allowed to fly free.

One day, a present arrived for the Emperor. It was a mechanical bird, made of gold and silver and precious jewels. When it was wound up with a golden key, the bird sang one of the nightingale's songs, moving its shining tail. It was a gift from the Emperor of Japan.

The mechanical bird sang very well, and what is more, it always sang exactly the same song, over and over again. The real nightingale sang as her heart told her, sometimes happily, sometimes sadly, sometimes loudly, sometimes softly.

"This mechanical bird will never disappoint you, Your Imperial Highness," said the Court Musician. "And she is much more beautiful than the real nightingale."

So it was generally agreed in the palace that the mechanical bird was preferable to the living songstress, which was just as well, for the real nightingale had taken advantage of the commotion to fly through the window and back to its old, free life in the forest.

Only the poor people, who were sometimes allowed to hear the mechanical bird, shook their heads and said to themselves, "No, there is something missing. This is not as beautiful as the real bird."

A year passed. The mechanical nightingale sat on a silken cushion on the Emperor's left side, which was a position of great privilege. But one day when the bird was wound up with the golden key as usual, it merely said, "Krrrrr. Krrrrr." The bird had sung so often that its mechanism was worn out.

Luckily, the Court Watchmaker was able to repair the bird, but he warned that in future she must only sing once a year.

Several years passed, and the people of China were shocked to learn that their Emperor was dangerously ill. He lay, pale and cold, on his magnificent bed. The courtiers were so sure that he was about to die that they began to pay court to the man who would be the next Emperor.

In the middle of the night, as the moonlight streamed through his open window, the Emperor was visited by fears and phantoms. "Sing!" he begged the mechanical nightingale at his side, hoping to drown out his dark thoughts. But there was no one to wind up the wonderful bird, so it remained silent.

Suddenly, through the open window, the Emperor heard a wonderful sound. It was the real nightingale, perched on a branch outside and singing her heart out. As she sang, the Emperor's fevered mind was soothed, and his illness left him.

"Thank you, little bird," he gasped. "I don't deserve your help after the way I treated you. But now you must remain in my palace and sing to me every day."

"No, My Lord," said the nightingale. "I cannot live in a palace, but I will come of my own free will and sing outside your window as often as I can. And I will do something more for you. I will tell you what the poorest people in your land are thinking and feeling—something that you cannot know, surrounded as you are by courtiers eager to impress you. But you must promise never to tell anyone what I am doing."

The Emperor promised gladly and fell into a deep, refreshing sleep. When the servants came at last to look at their dead Emperor, they found him alive and smiling, ready to take up the reins of power again.

The Emperor ruled for many more years, more wisely and well than ever before, but he kept the nightingale's secret to the end of his days.

THE UGLY DUCKLING

One sunny summer day, when the wildflowers were nodding in the heat, a mother duck sat on her nest. She had found a shady spot in some weeds at the edge of the pond.

It seemed to the duck that she had been sitting on her eggs for a very long time. Then, one morning, she heard a tiny sound from one of the eggs. Peep! Peep! A little duckling scuttled out from under her feathers.

All at once, there were little sounds from more of
the eggs. Before long, twelve fluffy little ducklings
were cuddling up to their mother.

"It's lovely to see you, my dears," she quacked.
"The wait has been so long." But one of the eggs—the
largest of all—had not yet hatched. "How annoying,"
said the mother duck, and she settled down to wait a
little longer.

Sure enough, a day or two later, there was a tap-
tapping from the egg. First a little beak appeared.
Then a little head peeked out. At last a funny little
bird stood in the nest.

Well! The mother duck could hardly bear to look
at the youngster. He really was the ugliest bird she had
ever seen. He didn't look like a duckling at all.

"I'll push him into the water," said the mother
duck. "If he cannot swim, I'll know he is a turkey or
some other kind of bird."

But when she nudged the untidy bird out into the pond, he swam off quite happily. In fact, he swam so well that the duck felt quite proud of her ugly duckling.

"Come along, my dears," she cried to her children, "and I will introduce you to the other animals in the barnyard. Just watch out for the cat!"

In the barnyard, the other ducks and the hens quacked and clucked in approval as the mother duck led her twelve little ducklings past. But when they saw the last duckling, they shook their heads and hissed and squawked.

"What a horrible bird!" they cried.

"He will grow into his feathers," replied the mother duck. "And I must tell you that he swims better than all my ducklings." She shepherded her brood back to the pond.

As the ducklings grew, they loved to swim and dive in the pond. Then they would waddle in the barnyard, shaking their feathers. But the ugly duckling soon dreaded the barnyard birds. They pecked at him and called him names. Every day it grew worse.

At last a morning came when the little duckling could bear it no longer. He ran and fluttered as fast as his legs could carry him away from the barnyard.

As night fell, he came, tired and hungry, to a wild marsh, where little frogs jumped and croaked in the moonlight. In the morning, the wild ducks who lived there found a stranger among them.

"We've never seen a duck as ugly as you!" they laughed. "But you can live here if you like, as long as you don't get in our way."

The little duckling was still lonely, but at least no one bullied him. Then one morning, as he swam by the bank, he suddenly saw a dog running through the reeds. All around the marsh, hunters and their dogs were gathering.

The little duckling hid in the reeds all day, trembling with fright as shots whistled over his bowed head.

That night, he once again fled as fast as he could from his unsafe home.

The weather was growing colder, and the wind was ruffling his feathers, when he came to a tumbledown cottage and crept inside to escape the coming storm.

An old woman lived in the cottage with her cat and her hen. She let the duckling stay, but the cat and hen were not very friendly.

"Can you lay eggs?" they asked. "Or purr, or catch mice?"

"No," whispered the duckling.

"Then you are no use at all," said the cat and hen.

At last, the duckling could bear the unkindness no longer. He wandered out into the world once more.

When the duckling came to a lake, he realized how much he had missed swimming. It was lovely to glide across the water in the moonlight. But winter was coming, and the nights grew colder.

One frosty day, at sunset, a flock of beautiful white birds flew over the lake. The duckling did not know that they were swans, but he longed to see them again. He felt that he had never seen anything so lovely.

The days grew colder and colder. One morning, the poor duckling woke to find that he had become trapped in the frozen water. Luckily, a passing farmer freed him and carried him home to his family.

But the youngster was frightened by the children's attempts to play with him. As he clumsily flapped his wings, he knocked over dishes and made a terrible mess. The farmer's wife chased him from the house.

Once again, the young bird was on his own. He struggled through the rest of the winter.

But gradually, the days became lighter. The grass began to grow, and spring flowers appeared. The bird found that his wings were stronger, and he could fly swiftly over the water. One afternoon, he caught sight of the beautiful white birds he loved so much far below.

"I must talk to them, just once," thought the young bird, "even if they attack me because I am so ugly."

As he landed, the swans rushed toward him, beating their wings. The bird bowed his head, waiting for their attack. As he did so, he saw his reflection. He wasn't an ugly duckling at all! Through the winter months he had grown up … into a beautiful white swan! The other swans had come to welcome him.

No bird was ever so happy, as he swam with his new friends. Later, two children came to feed the swans.

"Oh look," they cried, "there's a new one! And he's the most beautiful swan of all!"

THE SHADOW

Once there was a writer who went from a cold country to a hot one. He could not go out in the daytime, for it was just too hot. In the evening, when it was cooler, the streets were filled with people.

Opposite the man's home was a house that seemed to be empty, yet lovely music came from it. As he sat on his balcony one night, with the lighted room behind, the man saw that his shadow seemed to be sitting on the opposite balcony.

"If only you could go inside for me and see who is there," said the man. And, you know, when he got up and went inside, the shadow did look as though it went into the house opposite.

The next morning, the man was astonished to find that he had no shadow at all! At first he was worried about this, but after a few days he noticed that a new shadow was beginning to grow, and by the time he returned to his home in the cold country, the shadow was as long as it ever was.

Several years passed, and one evening, when the man was writing in his room, there was a knock at the door. Standing outside was a very thin man, who gave our hero goose pimples all over.

"I suppose you don't recognize me," said the visitor, "now that I have become so human. I am your old shadow. I have become rich and wise since I left you, but I wanted to see you again one more time."

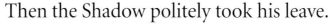

"But what happened to you?" asked the man in astonishment.

Then the Shadow described how he had entered the house opposite and found that a goddess named Poetry lived there.

"Even standing in the hallway, I found that it was as though I saw everything in the world and understood everything too," said the Shadow. "A great desire came upon me to be a man, but I had no clothes or money. The next day—don't laugh!—I hid under the baker woman's skirts and didn't come out until nighttime. Then I ran here and there, telling people truths about themselves that even they did not know. And they were so grateful and so afraid that their friends would find out that they gave me rich presents and the fine clothes you see me in today."

Then the Shadow politely took his leave.

A year passed, and the Shadow called on his old master again.

"Things are going even better for me," he said. "Look, I have grown quite plump. How are things with you?"

"I still write my books about goodness and beauty and truth," said the man, "but no one wants to read them."

"Listen," said the Shadow. "I feel like taking a trip and I would like a companion. Will you come with me —as my shadow?"

"That's crazy," said the man. "Of course not."

But the next year, the man became tired and ill.
"You look like a shadow!" said his friends.

When the Shadow called again, the man agreed
that a warmer climate would be good for his health.
So he set off with the Shadow, and stayed at his side all
the time, as a good shadow should.

At last the Shadow and *his* shadow reached a spa,
where people go to get better from illnesses. Also
staying there was a Princess, who saw very clearly.

"I know why you are here," she said to the
Shadow. "You cannot cast a real shadow!"

"That's nonsense," cried the Shadow. "Look, there
he is. I treat him so well, giving him clothes and food,
that he has become almost human."

So the Princess talked to the shadow-man, and
found him very intelligent.

Then the Princess thought, "I will marry this man
who is so extraordinary that even his shadow is wise."
And she took the Shadow to her own country.

As the wedding preparations were made, the Shadow said to the man, "Listen, I will give you money and a state coach if only you will always stay with me and never tell a soul that I was once your shadow."

"Never!" cried the man. "You are mad!"

Then the Shadow ran quickly to the girl, looking shocked and pale.

"Oh, a dreadful thing has happened," he told her. "My shadow has gone crazy and thinks he is human. I have had to have him locked away!"

"It might be better," said the Princess, "if he never appeared again."

So that night, when the wedding took place, the Shadow's shadow was not there, and he has never been seen since.

THE TINDERBOX

One fine day, a soldier met a witch upon the road. "If you will climb into the hollow in that tree for me," she said, "you will be a rich man. All I want is an old tinderbox that you will find in there."

The soldier had always wanted to be rich, so he agreed. Inside the tree, as the witch had told him, were three rooms. In each room was a chest of money, guarded by a fierce dog. The first had eyes as round as saucers. The second had eyes as big as mill wheels. The third had huge eyes, like round towers. But the witch had also told the soldier how to deal with the dogs, so he quickly filled his pockets and hat with money. Then, picking up the old tinderbox, he climbed out of the tree.

The soldier wondered why the witch wanted the tinderbox so badly, but she refused to tell him.

"You can cut off my head before I'll say a word," she said. So the soldier did!

After that, the soldier lived a wonderful life, with rich food and wine, handsome clothes and fine friends. But in a surprisingly short time, all his money was spent. Now he lived in an attic room, with only the stub of a candle for light.

One evening, the soldier felt in his pocket and found the old tinderbox. He thought he would use it to light his last candle. But as he struck a spark from the flint, the dog with eyes as round as saucers appeared before him. Two strikes, and the dog with eyes as big as mill wheels appeared. With three strikes, the soldier could summon the dog with huge eyes, like round towers. And the dogs were ready to do whatever the soldier asked, bringing him money, jewels, and other fine things.

Soon the soldier was as rich and happy as he had been before. One day, he heard that the King and Queen of the country had a beautiful daughter, but that she was hardly ever seen. Feeling curious, he sent the first dog to fetch her.

As soon as he saw the Princess, the soldier wanted more than anything to marry her. He kissed her and reluctantly sent her back to the palace.

The next morning, the Princess told the King and Queen that she had had a curious dream of being kissed by a soldier. At once, the royal pair decided to keep a close watch on their daughter.

Each night, the soldier could not help sending one of his dogs to fetch the Princess. It was not long before the King and Queen tracked him down. He was quickly thrown into prison and sentenced to death.

"If only I had my tinderbox with me," said the soldier. At last, he managed to give a message to a little boy outside his window, who ran off at once to fetch the tinderbox.

With the tinderbox in his hand once more, the soldier knew that nothing could hurt him. He summoned the three dogs, who quickly overpowered the guards and chased away the King and Queen, who had come to watch the execution.

The people were happy to offer the throne to the Princess, and she was happy to accept it—and the hand of the handsome soldier whose face she had seen in her dreams. So the soldier lived happily ever after, and the most pampered guests in the royal palace were … his dogs, of course!

THE FIR TREE

Once upon a time, a little fir tree grew in a forest. All around him were beautiful trees. The sunlight flecked his branches with gold, and the wind sighed around him. But the little fir tree was not happy. He longed to be bigger.

Time passed. Each year, the tree grew taller and his branches spread.

"Perhaps I will soon be cut down," he said, "as the biggest trees are each year. Then I will travel over the sea. How wonderful that will be!"

The storks had told the little tree
that the largest trees were
made into the masts of ships.
Each year at
Christmas time, some
smaller trees were cut
down, too.

"They are taken into
people's homes," said the
sparrows, "and decorated
with toys and jewels."

That sounded even better to the little fir tree,
although the sparrows did not seem to know what
happened to the trees after Christmas.

All this time, the fir tree could think of nothing
but growing bigger. He was very beautiful, but he
cared nothing for his lovely home and the blue sky
above. All he wanted was to be grown up and gone.

And, of course, the little tree did grow. The very
next Christmas, he was one of the first to be cut down.

Down in the town, the fir
tree was chosen by a very
grand family and carried
back to their magnificent
home. How proud he felt,
covered with candles,
ornaments, and presents.
But he was too busy
wondering what would
happen next to feel really happy.

That night, the children danced around the tree and opened their presents. It was such a pretty sight!

Next morning, some servants removed the rest of the decorations and put the tree away in a storeroom, with lots of old boxes and junk. Only the golden star on his highest branch remained.

The tree was lonely in the storeroom, until some little mice came to talk to him. They wanted to hear about his life in the open forest, and all that he had seen and done in the great house.

"How happy you must have been!" they cried.

"I suppose I was," said the fir tree. "But I did not feel happy then."

Some months later, when the fir tree was yellow and dry, he was taken out into the yard.

"Look at that ugly old tree!" cried the children, who were playing outside. They stamped on his brittle branches and broke them.

Then the tree realized how happy he had been in the storeroom, where no one had troubled him. But he had not felt happy at the time.

Before long, a servant came. He chopped up the tree for firewood. Piece by piece, the poor tree was burned on the kitchen stove.

"How happy I was in the yard," he sighed, giving off little crackles and pops as he was thrown into the flames.

At last all the tree was gone. Poor tree! In all his wonderful life, he had always been wishing for something else, and never felt truly happy. You won't be like him, will you?

THE BRAVE TIN SOLDIER

Once there was a box of twenty-five tin soldiers. They all looked exactly the same, with smart red and blue uniforms and rifles on their shoulders, except that the last one had only one leg, for the toymaker had run out of tin when he was made.

But the last tin soldier could stand up as straight as his brothers, and he was just as brave. At night, when their little owner had gone to bed, all the toys jumped up and played by themselves.

The last tin soldier looked all around, and he noticed a fine toy castle, with a lady at the door. He saw that she was very pretty, wearing a beautiful dress. And she only had one leg, too!

"She would make a fine wife for me," said the tin soldier, and he climbed up on a box so that he could see her more clearly.

In fact, the pretty lady was a dancer, standing on one leg. Her other leg was tucked under her skirts. The tin soldier did not know this, and he did not know that he was sitting on a jack-in-the-box! At midnight, the box burst open, and the soldier went flying over to the windowsill.

Next morning, when the windows were opened, the little soldier fell out! Down, down, he went, until he landed upside down with his rifle sticking into the pavement. Although his owner came down at once to look for him, he went sadly back indoors when it started to rain.

The rain was heavy, but it ended at last, and two boys coming down the street *did* see where the toy soldier had fallen.

"Let's make a paper boat," they said, "and send him off along the running water."

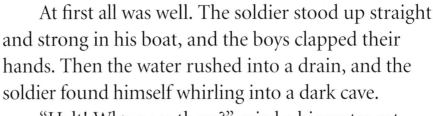

At first all was well. The soldier stood up straight and strong in his boat, and the boys clapped their hands. Then the water rushed into a drain, and the soldier found himself whirling into a dark cave.

"Halt! Who goes there?" cried a big water rat.

The soldier, having no choice, rushed on, with the water rat running behind him.

The noise of the rushing water became louder and louder. To his horror, the tin soldier saw that he was sailing toward a huge waterfall, where the water poured into the canal. Before he could do anything, the boat sank altogether, leaving the soldier floundering.

Just at that moment, a passing fish opened its jaws and … swallowed the soldier whole!

The tin soldier lay still inside the fish for a long time. Suddenly, he saw a flash of light and heard a cry. "The tin soldier!" The fish had been caught and taken to market. Now the cook who had bought it was cutting it open. And this was not just any cook! In five minutes, the tin soldier found himself back in the nursery with his brothers.

The tin soldier looked longingly at the pretty lady in the castle, for she had never left his heart. And she looked longingly at him.

But the soldier's adventures were not over. A little boy threw him into the fire. Brave to the last, the little man stood and felt himself melting. At that moment, a rush of air sent the pretty lady flying into the fire to join him. The soldier and his lady were together at last.

Next morning, when he raked out the fire, a servant found a tin heart—all that was left of the brave soldier and his lady love.

THE WILD SWANS

Once there was a King who had eleven sons and one little daughter, called Eliza. They were beautiful, happy children, although their mother had died many years before.

But one day, the King married a wicked Queen, who did not love the children. She sent Eliza to live with a poor family far from the palace and turned the boys into wild swans.

The years passed, and Eliza grew up to be both lovely and good. When she was fifteen, her father sent for her. As soon as she saw her pretty face, the wicked Queen hated Eliza even more. She stained the girl's skin and tangled her hair, so that her father, when he saw her, shuddered and sent her away.

Friendless and alone, the poor girl wandered
from the palace deep into the forest, where she bathed
in a crystal stream and became beautiful once more.
At night, under the trees, Eliza dreamed of her eleven
fine brothers, handsome and grown up now.

The next morning, Eliza met an old
woman on the path.

"Have you seen eleven fine Princes?"
she asked.

"No," replied the woman,
"but yesterday I saw eleven fine
swans with crowns on their heads
swimming along the stream."

Eliza followed the stream
to the sea. There she waited,
until at sunset eleven swans
with golden crowns came
flying toward her. Hiding
behind a bush, the girl
watched as the swans
landed. When darkness
came, each swan turned
into a handsome Prince
once more. With a cry,
Eliza ran to be reunited
with her brothers.

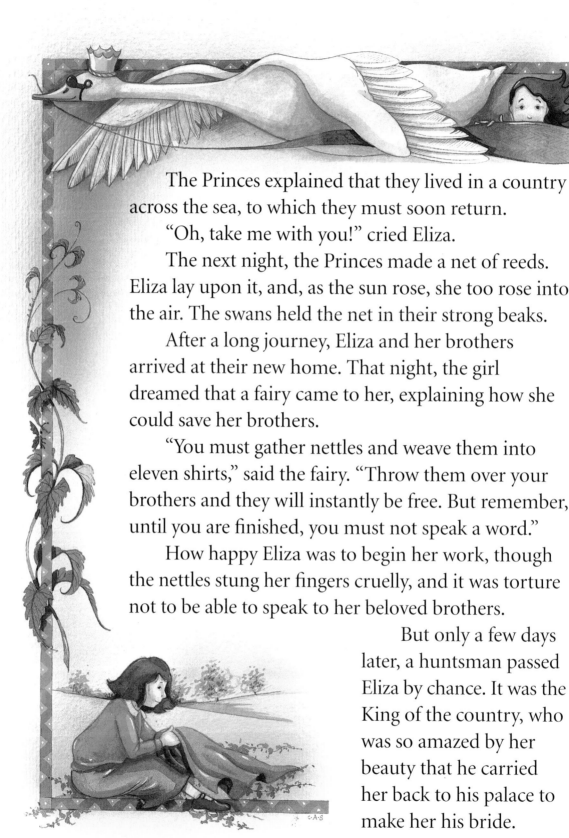

The Princes explained that they lived in a country across the sea, to which they must soon return.

"Oh, take me with you!" cried Eliza.

The next night, the Princes made a net of reeds. Eliza lay upon it, and, as the sun rose, she too rose into the air. The swans held the net in their strong beaks.

After a long journey, Eliza and her brothers arrived at their new home. That night, the girl dreamed that a fairy came to her, explaining how she could save her brothers.

"You must gather nettles and weave them into eleven shirts," said the fairy. "Throw them over your brothers and they will instantly be free. But remember, until you are finished, you must not speak a word."

How happy Eliza was to begin her work, though the nettles stung her fingers cruelly, and it was torture not to be able to speak to her beloved brothers.

But only a few days later, a huntsman passed Eliza by chance. It was the King of the country, who was so amazed by her beauty that he carried her back to his palace to make her his bride.

Eliza tried to escape, but she could not speak to explain her desperate task. Besides, she gradually grew fond of the King, who gave her a room of her own where she could work on the nettle shirts.

The time came when Eliza needed just one more bunch of nettles to finish the last shirts. She crept out of the palace in the dead of night and went to a nearby churchyard, where nettles grew. Unfortunately, the Archbishop, who had always mistrusted her, followed her. He believed that her visit showed she was a witch, and he persuaded the King to condemn her to death.

Alone in her prison cell, Eliza worked desperately to finish the shirts in time. At dawn, on the day of her execution, eleven beautiful swans flew down as she was led to the fire. In an instant, she threw the nettle shirts over them. Before the astonished eyes of the crowd and the King, the swans became Princes again, and Eliza could speak at last.

"I am innocent!" she cried.

Weeping with happiness, the King folded her in his arms, while her brothers gathered round. Only the youngest still had a swan's wing instead of an arm, for Eliza had been unable to finish her work before dawn.

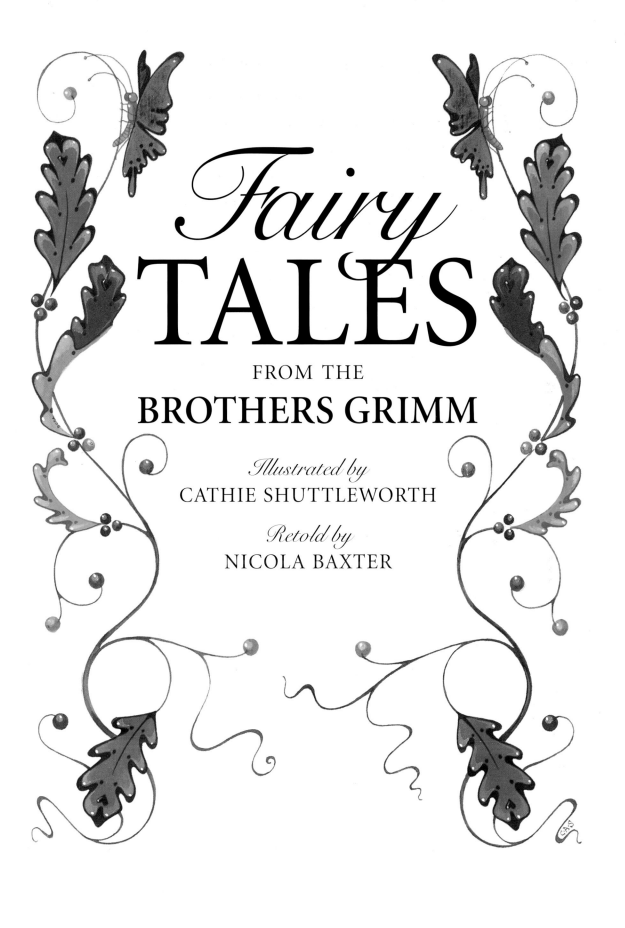

Fairy
TALES

FROM THE

BROTHERS GRIMM

Illustrated by
CATHIE SHUTTLEWORTH

Retold by
NICOLA BAXTER

HANSEL AND GRETEL

There was once a woodcutter whose beloved wife died, leaving him to bring up two little children. After a while, the woodcutter married again, but soon after that times became hard, and there was often not enough to eat in the woodcutter's cottage.

The new wife tried to make ends meet, but she soon became tired and sad. One evening, when the children were in bed, she spoke to the woodcutter.

"We do not have enough food for all four of us. Let's take the children into the forest and leave them there. Who knows, someone who will be able to take care of them better than we can may find them."

The woodcutter did not want to agree, but he could not think of another solution. Meanwhile, the woodcutter's children had been listening at the door.

"Don't worry, Gretel," said the little boy, whose name was Hansel. "I know how we can find our way home again."

The next day, the family went deep into the forest. As they walked, Hansel dropped crumbs from the crust of bread that he had saved for his lunch, hoping to follow them back home again. But the birds soon ate the crumbs, and when the children were left all alone in the forest, they were completely lost.

Hungry and afraid, Hansel and Gretel wandered through the trees. Suddenly, they saw a wonderful sight! A cottage made of candy and gingerbread!

But no sooner had the children munched into the house, than a sharp voice shouted from the window.

"Eat your fill, dear children, but you will pay for every bite. Ha, ha, ha!"

Before they knew what was happening, the children were bundled into the house by the witch who lived there.

"You will work for me, sweetheart," she said to Gretel, "but your dear brother will be a tasty dinner when he is a little fatter."

Every day, the witch asked Hansel to poke his finger out of the cage where she kept him, so that she could see if he was fat enough to eat, but Hansel held out a chicken bone to make her think that he was still just skin and bones himself.

At last the day came when the witch could wait no longer.

"Stoke up the fire, sweetheart," she said to Gretel, "and put your head in the oven to see if it is hot enough."

But Gretel did not trust the old witch.

"I don't know," she said. "You'd better check yourself."

No sooner had the witch poked her head in the oven, than Gretel gave her a huge push and slammed the door shut. Then she hurried to free Hansel.

Gathering up the witch's treasures, the children ran from the house, but they did not know which way to turn.

"Oh look!" said Hansel, suddenly. "It's one of the little birds that ate my crumbs. She is going to show us the way!"

The woodcutter could hardly believe his eyes when he
saw his children returning. His wife had left, and he was all
alone. When he saw the treasure that Hansel and Gretel
had taken from the witch's house, the woodcutter laughed.

"This will make us comfortable for the rest of our
lives," he said. "But you two are my real treasure, and I will
never lose you again."

SLEEPING BEAUTY

Once there lived a King and a Queen who had no children. When, at last, a baby daughter was born to them, they were overjoyed.

"I shall give the biggest and best feast ever seen for her," said her proud father.

It seemed as though everyone in the kingdom was invited. The most important guests were the twelve fairies who make special wishes for children. In fact, there were thirteen fairies in the kingdom, but in his excitement, the King forgot to invite the last one.

At the feast, the twelve fairies gave the little girl their best gifts: beauty and riches and goodness and much more.

Just as the eleventh fairy had finished her wish, there was a crash as the great door swung open. It was the thirteenth fairy!

"So you felt you didn't need me!" she screeched. "Here's *my* present! On her fifteenth birthday, the Princess will prick her finger on a spindle and die!" And she swept from the glittering room, as a terrible silence fell.

As the guests looked at each other in horror, the twelfth fairy spoke.

"I cannot take away the curse completely," she said, "but I can make it better. The Princess *will* prick her finger, but she will not die. Instead, she will fall asleep for a hundred years."

The years passed, as years do, and the Princess grew up to be clever and kind and beautiful, just as the fairies had promised. On the morning of her fifteenth birthday, she woke up early and walked out into the castle courtyard.

It was a beautiful day. As she walked, the Princess suddenly saw the sunlight glinting on a little door that she had never noticed before. She opened it and climbed eagerly up the winding stairs inside.

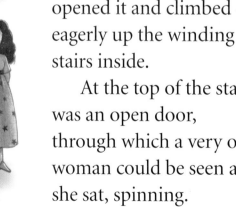

At the top of the stairs was an open door, through which a very old woman could be seen as she sat, spinning.

Now the Princess had never seen anyone spinning before, for the King had banished all spindles from the kingdom when he heard the thirteenth fairy's curse.

"What are you doing, good woman?" asked the Princess, politely.

"I am spinning this fine thread," answered the woman. "Would you like to try?" And she held the spindle out to the curious girl.

"*Oh!*" cried the Princess. As she took the spindle, she pricked her finger and immediately fell asleep.

At the same moment, everyone in the castle fell asleep. The King and the Queen slept in the throne room. The servants slept in the hall. Even the cook and the kitchen dogs fell into a deep sleep.

Many, many years later ~ exactly one hundred, in fact ~ a Prince happened to be passing the castle. It was so overgrown with brambles that you could only see the topmost turrets. But as he rode along beside the high, thorny hedge, the Prince saw something magical. Suddenly, the hedge burst into bloom! A thousand roses spread their petals in the sunshine, and the hedge opened to let the Prince through.

The Prince was astonished to see all the sleepers in the castle. At last, he found himself in the small room where the Princess herself was sleeping. He was so dazzled by her beauty that he bent over and kissed her.

At that moment, the hundred years came to an end. The Princess opened her eyes, and the first thing she saw was a handsome young man, smiling down at her. Gently, he led her from the room to the courtyard below, where the whole castle was coming to life.

It was not long before the Prince and Princess were married, and the King once more gave a great feast. But this time, he was very careful indeed with his invitations!

THE FROG PRINCE

Once upon a time, there was a King who had seven beautiful daughters. The youngest was the loveliest of them all.

On sunny days, the youngest Princess loved to play with her golden ball in a shady wood beside the castle. The sunlight sparkled through the leaves onto a cool pool nearby.

One day, when the Princess threw her golden ball high into the air, something dreadful happened. It fell … SPLASH! … into the water and sank to the bottom.

"It is lost forever!" the girl cried, but a croaky voice interrupted her.

"I could dive down and find your ball," said a little green frog by the pool, "if you would promise that I could be your friend, and share your meals, and snuggle into your little bed at night."

"Anything!" gasped the Princess hastily.

SPLISH! The frog dived into the water and soon reappeared with the golden ball.

The Princess was so delighted that she forgot all about her promise. She ran straight back to the palace, ignoring the little voice calling from the wood.

That evening, the King and his family sat down to supper. Just as they were about to start their meal, there came a croaking sound at the door. The youngest Princess tried to ignore it, but the King noticed that she looked pale.

"Who is there?" he asked.

Then the Princess explained about her promise. "But I can't let a horrible frog share my supper," she cried.

"A promise is a promise, my dear," said the King. "Let us meet your friend."

So, although the Princess shuddered every time she looked at him, the frog was allowed onto the table to share her supper.

After supper, the Princess tried to slip off to bed by herself.

"What about me?" croaked a little voice from the table. The Princess tried to pretend that she had not heard, but the King gave her a stern look.

"Remember what I said about promises," he said.

The Princess unwillingly carried the frog to her bedroom and put him down in a corner.

"I'd much rather sit on your pillow," croaked the little green creature.

Close to tears, the Princess picked up the frog and dropped him onto her pillow.

At once, the little green frog disappeared! In his place sat a handsome, smiling Prince.

"Don't be afraid," he said. "A wicked witch put a spell on me that only a kind Princess could break. I hope that we can still be friends, now that I am no longer a frog."

From that moment, the Prince and Princess became the very best of friends. In fact, a few years later, they had a wonderful wedding, and did not forget to invite some very special little green guests to join the celebrations.

THE FISHERMAN AND HIS WIFE

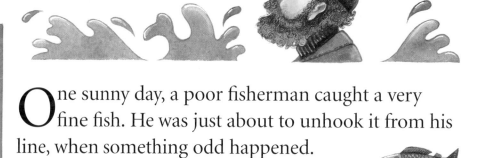

O ne sunny day, a poor fisherman caught a very
fine fish. He was just about to unhook it from his
line, when something odd happened.

"Please wait a moment," said the fish.

The fisherman rubbed his eyes. A fish that talked!
He must be dreaming.

But the beautiful silvery fish explained, "I am not
really a fish but an enchanted Prince. Please put me
back in the water."

"Of course," said the fisherman. "I wouldn't dream
of eating a talking fish!" He put the fish back in the sea
and went home to his wife.

The fisherman and his wife lived in a rickety old hut near the beach. It was in a terrible state! Everything was higgledy piggledy, and the place had not been cleaned for a very long time.

When the fisherman told his wife about the talking fish, she cried out, "You silly man! You should have asked for something for us in return. Go straight back and ask for a nice little cottage to live in."

So the fisherman went back to the seashore. The sun had disappeared behind a cloud.

When the fish heard the man's request, he wiggled his fins and said, "Of course. Your wish is granted."

The fisherman went home, but when he reached the place where his hut used to be, he saw a snug little cottage with roses around the door. And his wife was smiling all over her face.

But it was not long before the fisherman's wife began to have other ideas. After a couple of weeks, she nudged the fisherman one night and woke him up.

"I deserve better than this," she said. "Go back and ask that fish to give us a castle. I want to be Queen!"

The next day, much against his will, the fisherman did as she asked. There were waves washing angrily against the shore, and thunder was rumbling overhead, as the fish listened to his request.

"Very well," the fish replied. "Once more, your wish has been granted."

This time, when the fisherman trudged home, he found his wife surrounded by servants in an enormous castle. She seemed to be enjoying herself very much.

"You should bow to me, husband," she announced. "After all, I am the Queen."

It was only a few days later that the fisherman's wife frowned at him over the breakfast table.

"Being Queen is all very well," she said, "but I've been thinking…."

The fisherman's heart sank, as he set off for the seashore. The sea was dark and stormy. Huge waves crashed onto the sand, and lightning forked overhead.

"Oh fish!" called the fisherman. "My wife is tired of being Queen. Now she wants to be Empress of the Earth and Sky."

The fish's scales gleamed silver in the storm. "Go home," he said. "Your wife has all that she deserves."

And when he reached home, what did the fisherman find? Just a rickety old hut and his wife inside, complaining.

And although he goes down to the shore every morning, the fisherman has not seen the talking fish from that day to this.

THE ELVES AND THE SHOEMAKER

There was once a shoemaker who was so poor that he could not afford to buy enough leather to make shoes to sell. The day came when he had only enough left to make one pair of shoes. Very carefully, he cut out the leather and left the pieces on his workbench. Then, tired and sad, he went upstairs to bed.

The next morning, the shoemaker came downstairs to begin work. He was amazed to find that the leather had already been made into shoes. And they were so beautifully made that the shoemaker himself could not have done better.

The poor man could not understand what had happened, but he proudly put the shoes in his window. Within an hour, a very rich customer had seen the shoes and bought them. In fact, she was so delighted with them that she insisted on paying more than the shoemaker was asking!

"Now I have enough money to buy leather for *two* pairs of shoes," the shoemaker told his wife. "I will cut them out tonight and we shall see what happens."

The next morning, the shoemaker and his wife could hardly wait to creep down into the workshop. Sure enough, there on the workbench were *two* pairs of dainty shoes.

"I've never seen such fine workmanship," gasped the shoemaker.

Once again, he had no trouble in selling the shoes for a very handsome price.

From that day onward, the shoemaker's troubles were ended. Each evening, he cut out leather to make several pretty pairs of shoes. Each morning, he found the shoes standing ready on his workbench. Soon everyone knew where the finest shoes in town were to be found, and the shoemaker's shop was busy from morning till night.

One day, near Christmas, as the shoemaker closed the door on his last customer, his wife said, "I've been thinking, my dear, that we should try to find out who has been helping us all this time."

The shoemaker agreed. That night, instead of going to bed, he and his wife hid behind the workbench and waited to see what would happen.

As the clock struck midnight, the door opened and in danced two little men. They were dressed in rags and their feet were bare, but they cheerfully sat down and began to sew. Before dawn, they had finished their work and slipped out into the street.

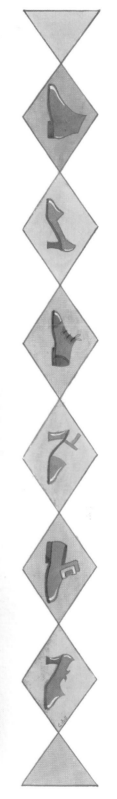

"So now we know," smiled the shoemaker. "What funny little men!"

"But did you notice, my dear, how old and torn their clothes were?" asked his wife. "Surely, the least we can do to thank them is to make them some new trousers, shirts and stockings. And you could make them some little shoes."

A few nights later, the tiny presents were finished. The shoemaker and his wife laid them on the workbench and hid as before.

Just after midnight, the little men reappeared. At the sight of the clothes waiting for them, they danced with happiness.

 "Now that we are such fine men,
We need not come to work again!"

they sang, and they skipped out of the shop, never to return.

The shoemaker and his wife were happy and wealthy for the rest of their days, but they never forgot the two little elves who gave them a helping hand.

THE MUSICIANS OF BREMEN

Once there was a donkey who worked very hard for his master. But when he became old and tired, he could no longer carry such large loads, and it became clear that his master would not keep him for much longer.

"The best thing for me to do," thought the donkey, "would be to take myself off before that day comes. I shall go to Bremen and become a musician. My braying has often been noticed."

So early one morning, the donkey set off for Bremen. On the way, he met a dog, sheltering by a tumbledown wall.

"You look rather sorry for yourself, old friend," said the donkey.

"I am too old to go hunting with my master," growled the dog. "Now, he hardly feeds me at all."

"Come with me to Bremen!" laughed the donkey. "If I bray and you bark, we shall make fine music!"

Off went the donkey and the dog. Before long, they met a cat, crouched on a roof.

"It's a fine morning!" called the donkey. But the cat meowed pitifully.

"Maybe it is for you," she called, "but I am old and even the mice laugh at me."

"Come with us and be a musician!" called the donkey and the dog. "Your voice is still strong and tuneful."

So the donkey and the dog and the cat went on their way to Bremen, singing as they went.

Now the musicians were making a very loud noise, but as they passed by a farmer's barn, they heard a noise that was so loud, it drowned even their strange and wonderful singing.

"Cock-a-doodle-doo! Cock-a-doodle-doo!"

"Goodness me," said the donkey. "This is a strange time of day for a rooster to be crowing."

"What else can I do?" called the rooster. "The farmer is having some friends to dinner tonight. I'm very much afraid that I'm the main course!"

"Don't worry," the donkey replied. "I can think of a much better use for your voice. You just come along with us."

And so the donkey and the dog and the cat and the rooster went on toward Bremen.

By the evening, the animals were tired. They needed a warm place to sleep and a fine dinner to end the day. At last, in the distance, they saw the lighted window of a little cottage.

When they reached it, the rooster flew up and looked in the window.

"I can see four robbers, sitting down to a delicious meal!" he called.

"That sounds just right for us," said the donkey. "And what is more, I have a plan."

So the dog climbed on the donkey's back. And the cat climbed on the dog's back. And the rooster perched on the cat's back. Then the animals went right up to the window and sang their music at the tops of their voices. It was an extraordinary sound!

"It's a ghost!" cried one robber, and rushed from the room.

"It's a goblin!" cried another, scrambling after him as fast as he could.

"It's a troll!" called the third, stumbling over his chair.

"I want my mother!" sobbed the last robber. "Wait for me!"

In just a few minutes, the four animal friends had taken the robbers' places at the table and were enjoying a delicious meal.

Later that night, the animals slept soundly in the warm, comfortable cottage. But the robbers had talked themselves out of their fear and crept back to see if the coast was clear. Luckily, the dog's sharp ears heard them coming, so the animals hid behind the door and waited silently in the darkness.

As soon as the robbers were inside the cottage, the donkey cried, "Now!" and took hold of one robber's trousers with his strong yellow teeth. In a flash, the dog had fastened his jaws around the second robber's ankles. The cat had jumped and sunk her claws into the third robber's shoulder. And the rooster had pecked the nose of the fourth robber so hard that it was never the same again.

Well, those robbers ran away even faster than they had the first time, leaving the four friends in peace. The cottage was so charming that they never did reach Bremen, but they made time for their singing practice every day. And if you had ever heard them, you would know that the good people of Bremen had a very lucky escape indeed!

LITTLE RED RIDING HOOD

Once there was a little girl who lived on the edge of a huge forest. The person she loved most in all the world was her grandmother, whose cottage was further along the forest path. One day, the old lady sent her granddaughter a beautiful red cape with a hood. The little girl loved it so much that she would *not* take it off! So that was why everyone called her Little Red Riding Hood.

One morning, Little Red Riding Hood's mother heard that the grandmother was not feeling well.

"Run along the forest path with this basket of food, Little Red Riding Hood," she said. "Your grandmother will feel better as soon as she sees you."

In no time at all, the little girl was ready to set off. She was wearing her red cape, of course.

"Now just remember," warned her mother, "you must go straight there and don't stop for *anything*."

"Don't worry," Little Red Riding Hood smiled, and off she went.

Now Little Red Riding Hood had not gone very far down the path, when out of the trees stepped a very large wolf!

"Why, Little Red Riding Hood," he said, "where are you off to in such a hurry?"

The little girl answered politely, "I am going to see my grandmother, but I'm afraid I *cannot* stop to talk." And on she went.

But when she was halfway to her grandmother's house, Little Red Riding Hood was surprised to see the same wolf leaning against a tree.

"I was just thinking, dear child," he said, "how nice it would be to take your grandmother some of the beautiful flowers that bloom by the path."

Well, that did seem to be a good idea, so Little Red Riding Hood stopped to gather the flowers. And when she looked up, the wolf was gone.

It was rather late by the time that Little Red Riding Hood knocked on her grandmother's door.

"Come in!" called a gruff voice.

"Poor grandmother, you don't sound well at all," cried the little girl.

Inside the cottage, Little Red Riding Hood tiptoed toward her grandmother's bed. The old lady did not *look* very well either!

"Why grandmother," gasped her granddaughter, not very politely, "what big ears you have!"

"The better to hear you with!" croaked the invalid.

Little Red Riding Hood crept closer still.

"Oh grandmother, what big eyes you have!" she cried in surprise.

"The better to see you with!" growled the figure in the big bed.

Little Red Riding Hood took one more step and had a dreadful shock.

"Oh grandmother, what big teeth you have!"

"The better to eat you with!" roared the wolf, jumping from the bed!

But just as the wolf was about to eat Little Red Riding Hood up in one enormous bite, a passing huntsman, who had heard the noise, rushed into the cottage.

"Aha!" he cried. "I've been looking for you, Mr. Wolf! Wait till I lay my hands on you!" And he chased the wolf right out of the cottage and into the trees.

Little Red Riding Hood was just recovering from her shock, when she heard a muffled sound from the cupboard. Bravely, she flung open the doors.

"Oh grandmother!" she cried with relief. "I thought you had been eaten up by that wicked wolf."

"He was saving me for dessert," said the old lady, hugging her granddaughter.

"And how are you feeling?" asked the little girl, remembering that her grandmother was not well.

"I *always* feel better when I see you, Little Red Riding Hood," smiled her grandmother. "You must know that!"

SNOW WHITE AND THE SEVEN DWARFS

One cold winter's day, a Queen sat sewing by an open window. Suddenly, she pricked her finger, and a drop of red blood fell on the snow below. The Queen looked down and sighed.

"One day," she whispered, "I would like to have a daughter with skin as white as this snow, lips as red as this blood, and hair as black as this window frame."

Before long, the Queen's wish came true. Her baby daughter looked just as she had imagined, so she called her Snow White. But very shortly afterward, the Queen died, leaving the baby to be brought up by her husband, the King.

The King was heartbroken by his wife's death, but he soon became lonely. Within a year, he had married again. The new Queen was extremely beautiful, but her heart was cold as ice.

Now the Queen had a magic mirror that she looked into every day. And every day she asked the mirror a question:

"Mirror, mirror,
On the wall,
Who is the fairest
One of all?"

The mirror would at once reply:

"O Queen, now I can truly say,
You are the fairest one this day."

Hearing this, the Queen would be satisfied.

Meanwhile, little Snow White was growing up. Every day she grew more and more beautiful.

So it was that the day came when the mirror gave a reply that made the Queen mad with fury.

"O Queen, your time has passed away,
Snow White is the fairest one this day."

Turning to look at her stepdaughter, the Queen saw the truth of the mirror's words. She hurried through the castle and called for a huntsman.

"Take Snow White into the forest," she told him, "and bring me back her heart to show that she is dead."

Reluctantly, the huntsman did as the wicked woman had said, but when the moment came to kill the girl, he could not bring himself to do it.

"Just leave me here," begged Snow White, sobbing. "I promise that I will never come home."

So the huntsman took back an animal's heart and left Snow White in the dark forest, all alone.

Snow White wandered through the trees for hours. Then, just when she thought she could go no farther, she saw a quaint little cottage. No one came to answer her knock, so she tiptoed inside.

What a curious little house it was! On the table were seven little plates and seven little glasses. In the middle was a basket of bread and fruit. Poor Snow White was so hungry that she took a little food. Then, she climbed up the winding stairs to the bedroom. There she lay down on the first little bed she came to and fell fast asleep.

Several hours later, Snow White was awoken by a sharp little voice.

"Just what do you think you are doing in our house?" it asked.

Snow White looked up to see seven dwarfs, in working clothes, standing around. The young girl took her courage in both hands and explained what had happened to her.

"And now," she said, "I have nowhere to go at all."

"Yes, you do!" chorused the dwarfs. "You can stay here with us!" They told her that they worked all day and needed someone to look after them.

"You will be safe here," they said. "But you must promise us never to open the door to a stranger."

So Snow White stayed
with the dwarfs. She cooked
their meals and cared for
their little house, but her life
was very different from the
one she had lived at home.
She longed for someone to
talk to during the long days.

Then, one fine morning,
her wish came true. An old woman, with a basket of
pretty things, knocked on the cottage door.

Snow White longed to look through the laces and
ribbons in the stranger's basket, but she remembered
her friends' warning. Still, she could not resist talking
to the woman through the open window.

Snow White did not realize that her visitor was none other than the wicked Queen in disguise. For months, the Queen had been so happy that she did not consult her mirror at all. When she did, she had a terrible shock.

"O Queen, you cannot have your will,
For Snow White is the fairest still."

Raging through her kingdom, the Queen had hunted high and low for the missing girl, taking on different disguises. She could scarcely hide her delight at finding her at last.

"You are wise not to open the door to strangers, my dear," she smiled. "But to show that there are no hard feelings, please take this shiny red apple as a gift from a new friend."

It seemed impolite to refuse, so Snow White stretched out her hand and took the apple. It looked delicious. Waving goodbye to her visitor, she took one tiny bite.

When the dwarfs returned from their work that evening, they found Snow White lying lifeless on the floor, the apple still clutched in her hand.

"This is the work of the Queen, I'm sure," cried one dwarf, sobbing. "She has robbed us of the sweetest girl in the world."

Sadly, the dwarfs took their friend and placed her in a crystal coffin, taking turns to watch over her night and day. She seemed to grow more lovely as she lay there, silent, cold and still.

One morning, a young Prince rode by and saw the coffin and the beautiful girl inside. He fell in love with her at once and vowed, although she could never be his bride, that he would not be parted from her.

"Let me take her back to my palace," he begged, "where she can lie in state as befits a Princess."

The dwarfs discussed the matter and agreed that she deserved no less. Carefully, they helped the Prince to lift the coffin.

But as they did so, the piece of apple that had caught in Snow White's throat was dislodged. She took one breath and then another. Amid the tears of her friends, she sat up and smiled at the Prince.

You may guess the end of the story. Snow White and her Prince lived happily ever after. And the wicked Queen? She was so eaten up with rage and envy that she died soon after, leaving the young couple to enjoy their happiness in peace.

RAPUNZEL

Once there lived a man and wife who wanted very much to have a child of their own. But year after year passed, and they did not have a baby. Often, the woman would sit sadly looking out of the window, from which she could see the garden next door.

Now this garden was very beautiful, full of flowers and vegetables, but no one dared to enter it because it belonged to a witch. One day, as the woman looked out, she suddenly had a great longing to eat one of the lettuces growing below.

"I feel as though I shall die if I do not have one of those delicious lettuces," she said to her husband. And she looked so pale and anxious that the poor man, much against his better judgment, agreed to go down and fetch her a lettuce.

That evening, as it was getting dark, the man crept over the wall and hurried toward the vegetable garden. He was just about to cut a beautiful lettuce when a voice crackled through the twilight.

"How dare you come into my garden to steal from me?"

The husband nearly jumped out of his skin. It was the witch! Stuttering with fright, he explained about his wife's great craving for lettuce.

"Very well," laughed the witch, "I'm not an unreasonable woman. You may take a lettuce, if you will give me your firstborn child in return."

The man was so frightened that he would have agreed to anything. And besides, he did not think that it was very likely that he would have children now, so he mumbled his thanks, took the lettuce, and ran.

But the strange thing was that only a few months later his wife gave birth to a beautiful baby daughter. Despite the pleadings of the mother and father, the witch made the man keep his promise. She took the child at once and gave her the name Rapunzel.

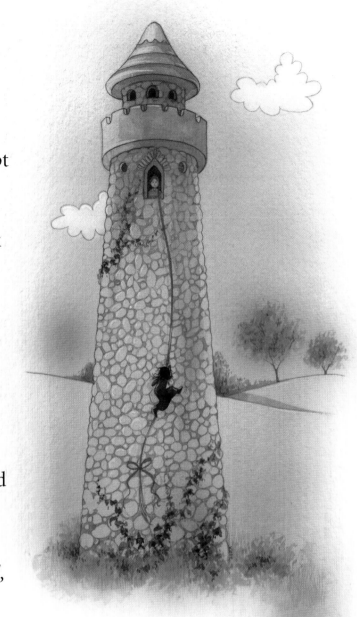

The little girl grew quickly and became more lovely every day. The witch was very kind to her and treated her like her own child, except for one thing. When Rapunzel was twelve years old, the witch took her to a high tower and put her in a room at the very top. There was no door and no stairs – just a small window for Rapunzel to look out from.

When the witch wished to visit, she stood at the bottom of the tower and called out,

"Rapunzel, Rapunzel,
Let down your hair!"

At this, the girl would lower her long, braided hair from the window, and the witch would climb up.

A few years later, a Prince came riding past and heard a beautiful voice singing from the top of the tower. Puzzled, he hid behind some bushes and waited to see what would happen. Of course, before long, the witch visited Rapunzel in her usual way.

As soon as the witch had gone, the Prince came out of his hiding place and called out,

"Rapunzel, Rapunzel,
Let down your hair!"

Thinking that the witch had returned, Rapunzel did as she was asked. She was astonished to see a tall, handsome young man climbing through the high window instead.

"Don't be afraid," he said. "I heard your beautiful singing and longed to see you for myself. Now I know that you are as lovely as your voice."

The Prince spoke kindly to the girl and, as she grew to know him, she grew to love him.

All went well until one day when the witch was visiting. As she climbed into the tower, Rapunzel spoke without thinking.

"Why is it, Mother dear, that you feel so much heavier than the Prince does, when he climbs up?"

There was an awful silence. Then the witch flew into such a rage that the stones of the tower trembled. She took out some scissors and snipped off Rapunzel's long braid. With her magic powers, she banished the frightened girl to a desert far away. Then, as the sun went down, she crouched near the window and waited.

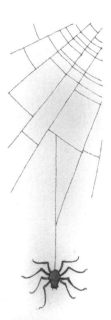

Before long, a voice drifted up from below.

"Rapunzel, Rapunzel,
Let down your hair!"

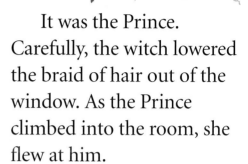

It was the Prince. Carefully, the witch lowered the braid of hair out of the window. As the Prince climbed into the room, she flew at him.

"I wanted to keep my darling safe from such as you!" she spat. And with a huge push, she hurled him to the ground.

The Prince fell like a stone into some bushes at the foot of the tower. He managed to stagger to his feet, but his eyes had been scratched by thorns, and he could not see at all. In darkness as black as his despairing thoughts, he stumbled away to a life of ceaseless wandering.

Years later, the Prince
came to the desert where
Rapunzel was living. In
the distance, he heard a
sound he thought that
he would never hear
again. It was the
sweetest voice
in the world,
singing
sadly.

"Rapunzel!" cried the Prince, running forward.
The poor girl was so overjoyed that she covered his
face with kisses and tears. As they fell onto the Prince's
eyes, the tears healed his wounds. Once more he could
see the girl he loved.

The Prince and Rapunzel returned to his
kingdom, where they lived happily together for the
rest of their days. The witch has never been heard of
since ~ but it would be wise never to take as much as a
petal, the next time you visit a beautiful garden.

THE TWELVE DANCING PRINCESSES

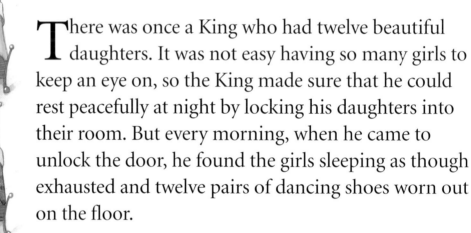

There was once a King who had twelve beautiful daughters. It was not easy having so many girls to keep an eye on, so the King made sure that he could rest peacefully at night by locking his daughters into their room. But every morning, when he came to unlock the door, he found the girls sleeping as though exhausted and twelve pairs of dancing shoes worn out on the floor.

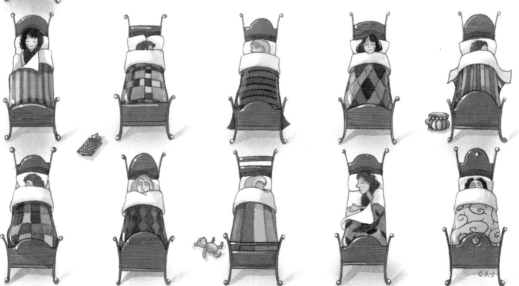

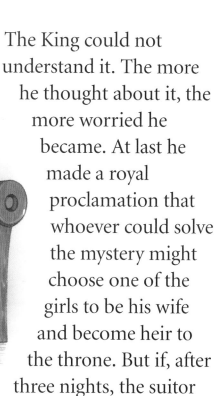

The King could not understand it. The more he thought about it, the more worried he became. At last he made a royal proclamation that whoever could solve the mystery might choose one of the girls to be his wife and become heir to the throne. But if, after three nights, the suitor was no nearer to the truth, then he must lose his life.

Several Princes came to try. They took up their posts in the hallway outside the Princesses' room and waited to see who came in. But one by one, they fell asleep and saw nothing at all. And one by one, they lost their heads.

One day, a wounded soldier passed through the kingdom. An old woman by the side of the road asked him where he was going.

Joking, the soldier replied, "Oh, I've nothing better to do, so I'm going to find out what happens to the Princesses' dancing shoes, night after night!"

The old woman looked at him for a moment and answered, "If you are serious, that is not so difficult. You must simply leave the glass of wine that is given to you in the evening, for it is drugged. Pretend to be asleep instead. Then, when the Princesses go dancing, put on this magic cloak. It will make you invisible, so that you can follow them wherever they go."

The soldier took the cloak and the advice and went on his way.

When the soldier presented himself at the palace, he was welcomed as politely as the earlier suitors. That night, he was given fine clothes to wear and shown to his bed in the hallway. The eldest Princess brought him a glass of wine, but he was careful only to pretend to drink it. Then he lay down and snored loudly to show that he was asleep.

As soon as they heard his snores, the Princesses put on their finest party clothes and jewels. They took out brand new dancing shoes and put them on their dainty feet.

Then the eldest Princess went to the head of her bed and pressed a secret panel. A passageway opened up behind it. One by one, the Princesses disappeared through the panel.

The soldier had watched all of this. Quickly, he threw on the magic cloak and went after the girls.

But in his hurry, as he followed them down the stairs, the soldier stepped on the hem of the youngest Princess's dress.

"What was that?" she cried. "Someone caught hold of me!"

"Don't be silly," the oldest Princess replied. "Come along!"

Before long, the Princesses reached the bottom of
the stairs and came to an avenue of beautiful trees.
Their leaves were silver and gold, gleaming in the
moonlight.

"I must take some proof that I was here," thought
the soldier. And he broke a twig from the nearest tree.

"What was that?" The youngest Princess heard the
tiny sound.

But the eldest Princess told her to be quiet.

"Hurry along," she said. "Our Princes are waiting
for us."

Next the Princesses came to an avenue of trees with diamond leaves. They sparkled and shimmered so brightly that the soldier could hardly see. Once again, he broke off a twig as evidence.

"I heard something again, I'm sure of it," whispered the youngest Princess. But once more her sister silenced her.

At last they came to a lake where twelve boats were waiting. And in each boat there was a handsome Prince. As the Princesses climbed in, the soldier joined the youngest Princess and her partner, but of course they could not see him.

"The boat feels heavy tonight," panted the Prince, as he rowed.

Across the lake stood a wonderful castle, brightly lit. From its open doors the sound of music streamed out over the water.

Laughing and talking, the Princesses and their Princes hurried inside, where they were soon swept away by the waves of music. As they danced around the floor, the soldier danced too, but no one could see him at all.

By three o'clock in the morning, the Princesses'
shoes were quite worn out. Saying goodbye to their
Princes, they hurried back to their room in the palace.

This time, the soldier went ahead of them. When
the sleepy Princesses reached their beds, he was once
again snoring in the hallway.

For two more nights, the soldier followed the
Princesses. On the third night, instead of twigs from
the sparkling trees, he brought back a golden goblet.

Next morning, he appeared before the court.

"Well," said the King, "have you found the answer
to the mystery?"

"I certainly have," said the soldier, and he
proceeded to tell the whole court about the secret
passage, and the magic trees, and the lake, and the
castle, and the dancing Princesses.

"And here," he said,
producing the twigs and
the goblet, "is my proof."

The King turned sternly to his daughters. "Is this true?" he asked.

Seeing that there was no way out, the girls confessed to their nightly journeys.

"Then you may choose whichever one of these troublesome girls you would like for your bride," the King told the soldier.

"I am not so young myself," the suitor laughed. "I will choose the eldest, who was so certain that there was no one following. But I am sure that all of her sisters will gladly dance at our wedding!"

So it was that a poor soldier became a great man and later King of the whole land.

KING THROSTLEBEARD

There was once a King who had a very beautiful daughter. Although she was the loveliest girl in the whole kingdom, and queues of suitors presented themselves every year, her heart was cold and proud. She laughed at all of them and sent them away.

"Very well," said her father, "I will sort this out once and for all. I will invite every eligible nobleman from far and near to a great feast. When you see them together, you are sure to find someone that you like."

So every King, Prince, Duke, Marquis, Earl and Baron came from hundreds of miles around. They were lined up in the great hall, and the Princess walked up and down the rows looking at them each in turn, like a general inspecting his troops!

"Ho, ho, ho! Look at his skinny legs!" she laughed, as she passed one very learned Prince.

"Ha, ha, ha! He looks like a frog!" she giggled, as she looked down at a very kind and hardworking Duke.

It was the same all the way down the line, until she came to a young King who was charming in every way. Still, there was something about his face that reminded the Princess of a bright-eyed bird.

"I'll call you King Throstlebeard," she chuckled. "I couldn't possibly marry someone so birdbrained! Ha, ha, ha!"

Seeing that she had rejected every suitor in the most unkind way, the Princess's father soon grew very angry with her.

"You will marry the first beggar who comes to the palace gates," he declared. "Then you will be sorry."

A few days later, a strolling player sat below the King's window and sang a haunting song. The King at once asked for him to be brought into the castle.

"Your singing has brought you a greater reward than you could imagine," he said. "Here is my daughter. She shall be your wife."

Despite the Princess's protests, she was married at once, and ushered out of the palace to make her way in the world with her new husband.

The Princess and the beggar trudged along through some beautiful countryside. The Princess wondered whose land could be so pleasing. Her husband laughed and replied,

"King Throstlebeard owns all both far and near.
You could have shared in everything that's here."

Then the Princess began to wish that she had not been so hasty. But it was too late now.

All day they walked along, and everywhere there were fine towns and well-tended farms. Each time she asked, the beggar told the Princess that all of this belonged to King Throstlebeard.

"I have been a fool," moaned the Princess. "If only I had married him!"

At this, the beggar became angry.

"You have been married to me for less than a day," he said, "and already you are wishing for another husband. Am I so unworthy of you?"

Before she could reply, the Princess saw that they had stopped at a tiny hut.

"This is my home," the beggar told his wife, "where you and I shall live together."

"But where do the servants live?" she asked.

"What servants?" chuckled the beggar. "You will be doing all the work around here, my dear."

So the Princess's new life began, but things did not go smoothly. She was no good at cooking or cleaning or washing the clothes. She could not make baskets or spin thread.

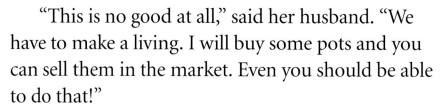

"This is no good at all," said her husband. "We have to make a living. I will buy some pots and you can sell them in the market. Even you should be able to do that!"

"But someone who knows me might see me!" wailed the Princess.

"So they might," replied her husband with a smile.

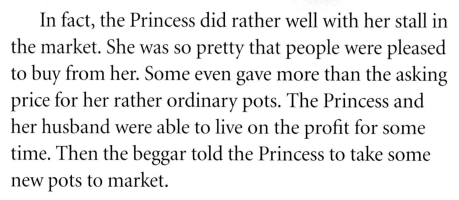

In fact, the Princess did rather well with her stall in the market. She was so pretty that people were pleased to buy from her. Some even gave more than the asking price for her rather ordinary pots. The Princess and her husband were able to live on the profit for some time. Then the beggar told the Princess to take some new pots to market.

This time, things did not go so well. The Princess set up her stall on a corner. Before an hour had passed, a runaway horse crashed into the stall and broke every pot that she had.

Of course, the Princess's husband was furious.

"You are completely useless," he said. "I cannot afford to keep you. But there is a post for a kitchen maid at the palace. They will feed you and you can bring home some scraps for me too."

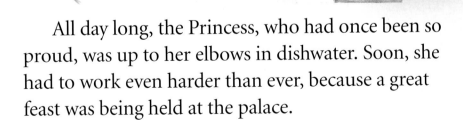

All day long, the Princess, who had once been so proud, was up to her elbows in dishwater. Soon, she had to work even harder than ever, because a great feast was being held at the palace.

That day, as she passed down a passageway, the Princess paused to peer through a door into the ballroom. It was full of beautiful people in fine clothes, reminding her of all that she had lost.

"It is my own fault," she admitted. "If I had not been so proud, I could have led a wonderful life."

At that moment, the King came into the room. To the Princess's horror, she realized that it was King Throstlebeard, whom she had rejected. Yet the King came straight toward the pretty girl and swept her, rags and all, into the dance. As he did so, the jars of scraps that she had saved fell out of the Princess's pockets and rolled across the floor.

The whole company roared with laughter at the sight, while the poor girl wished that the floor would open and swallow her up.

As she fled from the ballroom, the Princess found her way blocked by a man at the door. To her amazement, this was also King Throstlebeard!

"Don't be afraid," he said kindly. "I have taken on many forms, including the beggar whom you married. I see that you have learned to give up your pride and coldness. Now I am proud to make you my Queen."

From that day forward, the new Queen was the happiest woman in the world, and her kindness to everyone was known throughout the land.

RUMPELSTILTSKIN

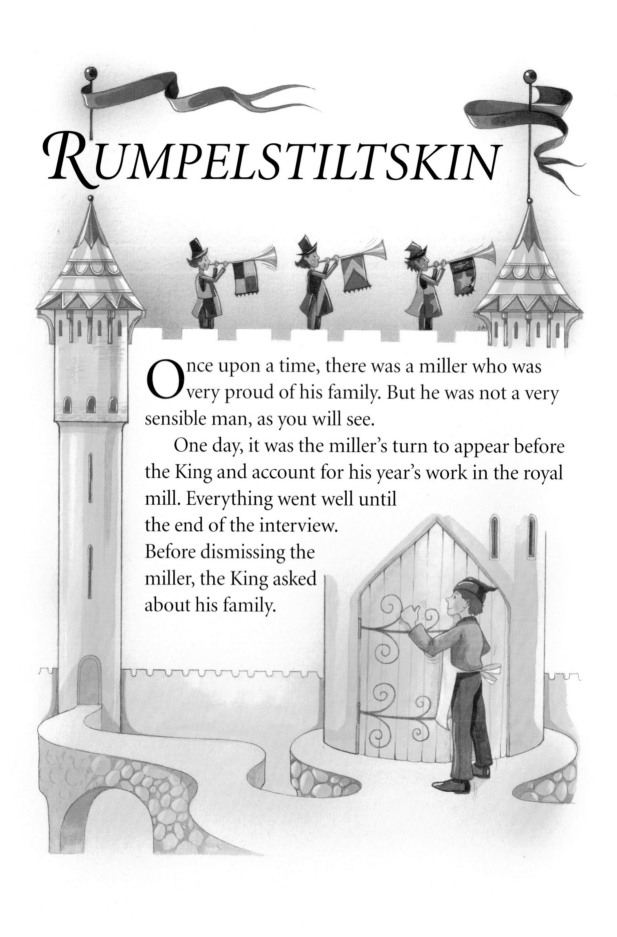

Once upon a time, there was a miller who was very proud of his family. But he was not a very sensible man, as you will see.

One day, it was the miller's turn to appear before the King and account for his year's work in the royal mill. Everything went well until the end of the interview. Before dismissing the miller, the King asked about his family.

"I hear that you have a very pretty daughter," said the King.

"Not just pretty, Your Majesty," cried the miller with pride. "Why, she is the cleverest girl in the kingdom as well!"

"Really?" said the King. "Tell me, what can she do that is so clever?"

"She … she … she … can spin straw into gold!" blurted out the foolish miller. He had said the very first thing that came into his head.

The King looked hard at the miller. He was very fond of money. It seemed unlikely that the girl could do as her father said, but it was worth a try.

"Bring her to the palace," said the King. "And I mean *right* away!"

So the miller went home and fetched his daughter. The King could not help noticing that she was a very pretty girl, but his mind was full of visions of gleaming gold. He took the girl to a small room, containing a spinning wheel and a huge heap of straw.

"Spin that into gold before dawn," said the King, locking the door, "or it will be the worse for you."

The girl began to cry. She had no idea what to do. Suddenly, through her tears, she saw that she was no longer alone. A strange little man stood before her.

"I may be able to help you," he said with a crafty smile, "but, of course, I will need something from you in return."

The hope that had brightened the girl's eyes for a moment faded away. "I have nothing to give you," she said.

Her visitor's sharp little eyes twinkled greedily. "Your pretty glass necklace will be payment enough," he said, and at once he set to work.

While the poor girl cried herself to sleep, the little man worked at the spinning wheel. All night long, it whirred and hummed. Before dawn, the strange little man had vanished as suddenly as he had arrived.

When he opened the door, the King was amazed
and delighted to see a pile of golden thread where the
straw had been.

"Tonight," he said, "I will give you a larger pile of
straw. We must test your skills again."

That night, the little man once again appeared to
help the bewildered girl. This time, he took the ring
from her finger as payment.

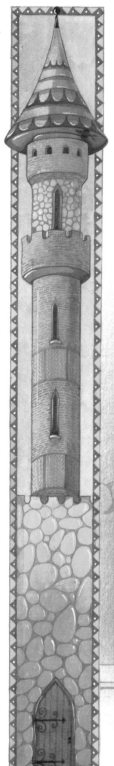

The King was a happy man. The next night, he showed the miller's daughter into an even larger room in a tower.

"If you complete your task again before morning," he said, "I will make you my Queen."

Once more, the strange little man appeared, but this time the poor girl sobbed her heart out.

"I have nothing left to give you," she explained. "Nothing at all."

The little man thought for a moment. "When you are Queen," he said, "you can give me your firstborn child instead."

What choice did the desperate girl have? Once again, the little man worked through the night.

The next morning, there was great rejoicing in the castle. The King announced his wedding to the pretty girl who had won his heart, and the miller was quite overcome with pride.

A year later, the happy young Queen rocked her first child gently in her arms. She was thinking only of the future. Suddenly, the strange little man of the year before appeared before her.

"I have come to remind you of your promise," he said.

The Queen begged him to take her jewels instead of her child, but the little man shook his head.

"I will give you one more chance," he grinned. "If you can guess my name before three nights have passed, you can keep your baby."

At once, the Queen sent out messengers to find the strangest names in the kingdom, and for the next two nights she tried every name she could think of ~ without success.

On the third night, a soldier came to her with an odd story.

"As I was riding through a wood," he said, "I saw a strange little man dancing around a fire and singing:

'The Queen can never win my game,
Rumpelstiltskin is my name!'"

That night, when the little man appeared, the Queen said, "Is your name Hibblehob?"

"No!" he yelled.

"Is it Grigglegreggers?"

"No, no, no!"

"Well, is it … Rumpelstiltskin?"

The little man went red in the face. He whizzed around and around in fury and stamped his foot so hard that he disappeared right through the floor!

And, you know, no one has seen that strange little man from that day to this.